WE ALL FALL DOWN

ALSO BY ERIC WALTERS

Shattered
Elixir
Triple Threat
Camp 30
Grind
The True Story of Santa Claus
Juice
Run
Overdrive
I've Got an Idea
Underdog
Death by Exposure
Royal Ransom
Off Season
Camp X
Road Trip
Tiger Town
The Bully Boys
Long Shot
Ricky
Tiger in Trouble
Hoop Crazy
Rebound
The Hydrofoil Mystery
Full Court Press
Caged Eagles
The Money Pit Mystery
Three on Three
Visions
Tiger by the Tail
Northern Exposures
War of the Eagles
Stranded
Trapped in Ice
Diamonds in the Rough
Stars
Stand Your Ground

a novel by ERIC WALTERS

WE ALL FALL DOWN

WE ALL FALL DOWN
Seal Books/published by arrangement with Doubleday Canada
Doubleday Canada edition published 2006
Seal Books edition published January 2007

ISBN-13: 978-0-7704-2992-8
ISBN-10: 0-7704-2992-0

Cover design: CS Richardson
Cover image: Chad Baker/Getty Images

Seal Books are published by Random House of Canada Limited.
"Seal Books" and the portrayal of a seal are the property of
Random House of Canada Limited.

Visit Random House of Canada Limited's website:
www.randomhouse.ca

PRINTED AND BOUND IN THE USA

OPM 10 9 8 7 6 5 4 3 2

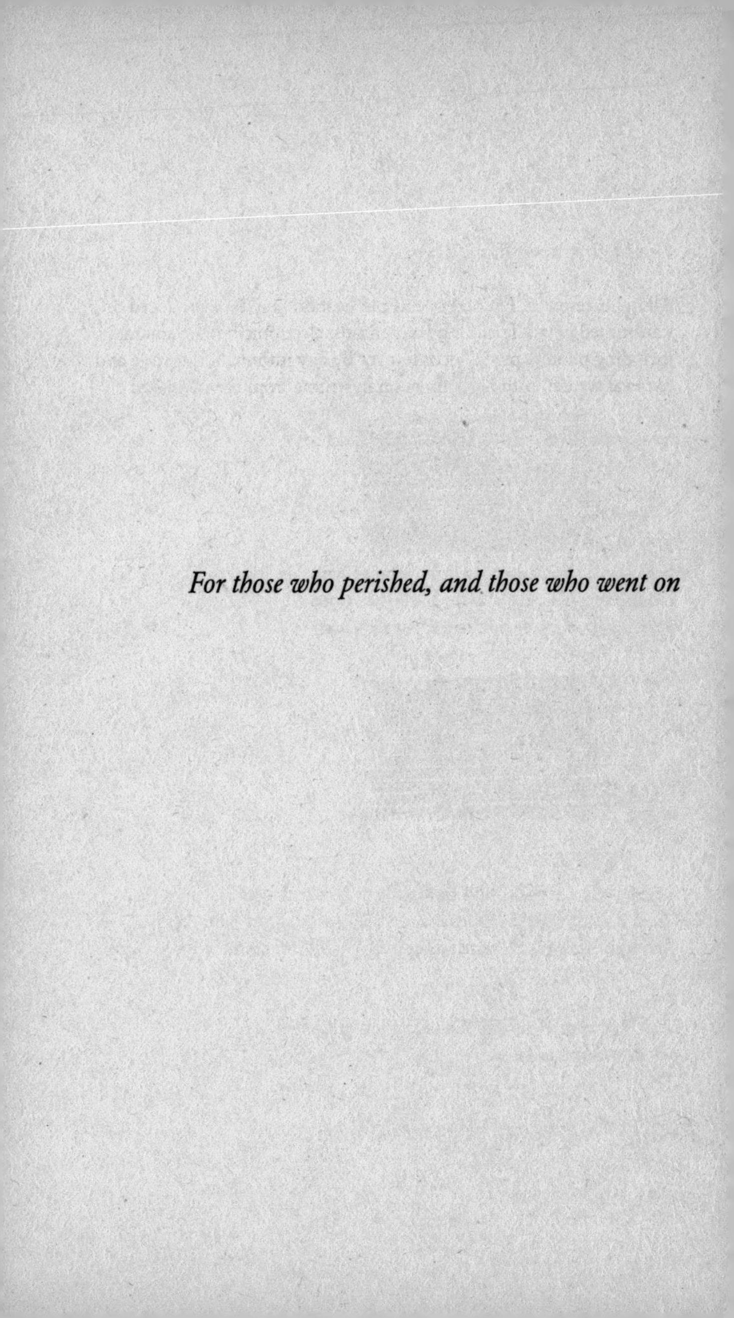

For those who perished, and those who went on

CHAPTER
ONE

"Okay, everybody, let's settle down and get to work!" Mrs. Phelps, my history teacher, yelled out over the din of the class.

Slowly, reluctantly, people ended their conversations and shuffled to their seats. Monday morning at 8:30 was not a great time to do anything except sleep. Up until last week, that's what I *was* doing at this time. I still couldn't believe how fast the summer holidays had gone by.

While there were no assigned seats I slipped into my usual spot, like everybody else. It was amazing how quickly–within a few days–everybody had fallen into predictable patterns. Not that

I was complaining, because I had a good seat–not by the front, but not in the very back row, either. Teachers always kept a close eye on anybody who sat in the last row. On my left-hand side was my best friend, James. Beside him, clearly visible as I innocently looked in his direction to talk, was a girl who had lots of cleavage, wore little tiny tops and had a tendency to bend over a lot to get things out of the pack underneath her desk. Actually, this was a *very* good seat.

"You'll have to excuse me if I still don't know all of your names," Mrs. Phelps said.

I figured her not knowing mine was still a plus.

"I have four grade nine history classes this semester, so that's over one hundred students who are new to the school and new to me."

I didn't know Mrs. Phelps very well yet, but I liked her. She was interested in her students, but not too interested. And she seemed to take her job seriously, but not too seriously. She wore a wedding ring, and there were pictures of a couple of kids on her desk. That meant she had a life beyond history. Teachers who lived for their subject could really make their students' lives miserable.

This school was so much bigger than my old school. It was hard to go from being the big guys in grade eight to being the little kids in grade nine. High school was like a whole different world–a world inhabited by thousands and thousands of kids I didn't know, all of whom seemed a whole lot bigger than me. Thank goodness almost all of my class from the old school had made the transfer, so I knew lots of people already. Actually, people like James I'd known since *Kindergarten*. Good old James. I looked over and past him to that girl . . . wow . . . maybe there was nothing wrong with getting to know new people, either.

"I'm going to recite a line of poetry and I want you all to say the next line."

There was an audible grumbling and I turned to James to ask if I'd missed a poem in the assigned reading. Suddenly my attention was caught as that girl slowly reached underneath the desk for her history textbook. My mouth dropped open and I tried not to stare . . . I wondered if she was doing that by accident or if it was a very deliberate thing meant to drive boys–to drive *me*–crazy.

"*Ring around the rosie*!" Mrs. Phelps sang out.

"*A pocket full of posies*," most of us chanted back after a slight hesitation.

"*Ashes, ashes*," she continued.

"*We all fall down*," we all said, finishing the rhyme.

"Excellent! So you all know that poem."

"Poem? Isn't that like a nursery rhyme?" somebody asked.

"Rhyme, as in poem," Mrs. Phelps replied. "Since this is a history class, can anybody tell me the *history* of this verse?"

"I think my mother taught it to me, so it must be pretty old," a girl said.

I realized that with the exception of a few kids in the class it wasn't just Mrs. Phelps who didn't know people's names.

"It *is* very old. Even older than your mother or grandmother, or great-grandmother," Mrs. Phelps said.

"And it's English, right?" a second girl said–or really asked.

"Old English. Very old. This poem is believed to be somewhere between six and seven hundred years old."

That surprised me, and judging from the looks and murmurs from the rest of the class I wasn't alone.

"Does anybody know what this verse means?"

"It's something kids say when they play games or skip," the first girl replied.

"Yeah, they played a lot of games back then because they didn't have TV or radios or even video games," a guy added. "All they had was, like, rocks . . . I think that's why they called it the Stone Age."

"Actually, the time frame when that verse was written is most commonly called the Dark Ages, but you're correct, they didn't have anything that we would consider modern," Mrs. Phelps said.

I was impressed by how gently she'd said that, instead of just telling him that he was stupid.

"And the rhyme became popular because of the absence of some other modern amenities . . . primarily health care, medicine and proper sanitation. Many people believe that the poem that you all knew and recited is about the bubonic plague, about the Black Death."

James leaned over and gave me a little nudge. "Black Death . . . how about that for a name for the group?" he whispered.

I shook my head. We weren't black, and I was seriously hoping that nobody would die. James played guitar and I played bass and saxophone. We'd been jamming with a couple of other guys in James's garage, and we were trying to come up with a name for our band.

"I'll translate the poem for you," Mrs. Phelps said. "The first line, *Ring around the rosie*, refers to the rose-colored discoloration of the skin and flesh caused by the plague. The skin turns purple and then black, most often in the extremities . . . fingers, toes and, in males, the genitalia."

I felt a shudder go up my spine as an audible groan came from the males in the room. Somehow that last part seemed a lot worse than your fingers and toes changing color.

"*A pocket full of posies*," Mrs. Phelps continued. "This refers to the sweet-smelling flowers that those who were tending to the sick would carry to help ward off the stench of the disease and deaths."

"I read somewhere that was why brides originally started to carry flowers at weddings, to cover up how they smelled, because nobody ever took baths in the olden days," a girl said.

"Fresh water, especially heated fresh water, was certainly uncommon, especially in the cities during the Dark Ages. But the smell from the plague would be much worse than that caused by simply not washing. Imagine the stench caused by rotting meat, human body parts that were dying while the patient remained alive."

I tried hard *not* to imagine that but wasn't successful.

"The line, *Ashes, ashes*, is about the impending death," Mrs. Phelps said. "Although there is an alternative line: *A-choo, a-choo*. This signifies the sneezing and coughing of the pneumonic form of the plague, the type that is in the lungs. And the final line, *We all fall down*, simply refers to death." She paused and took a sip from her coffee mug.

"Although there is still some debate among historians, it is believed that while there have been countless epidemics, there have been only three major pandemics. In a pandemic, a disease affects not just a local area but a broad geographic region–maybe a whole continent. The first pandemic spread from the Middle East to the Mediterranean Basin in the fifth and sixth centuries and killed half the population of the affected areas. Think about that number. Now, look around the room."

I looked over at James and, of course, past him. I had to try to talk to her and try to remember to keep my eyes meeting her eyes and no place else. That wouldn't be easy.

"I want everybody born in January through June to stand up," Mrs. Phelps said.

I was born in March and got to my feet. James was a July baby and stayed seated. The girl–I *had* to find out her name–rose as well. What if we shared a birth month? Maybe that would give me an excuse to talk to her.

"About half of you are on your feet. All of those standing would be dead."

"If you're dead, can I have your iPod?" James asked.

"If I'm dead I can't say yes."

"If you're dead you can't say no," James said, and a bunch of people laughed.

"Everybody take your seats again. The second pandemic occurred between the eighth and fourteenth centuries and affected almost all of Europe, resulting in a 40 percent mortality rate. Finally, the last pandemic was in 1855, starting in China and spreading to all the continents except Australia and Antarctica."

"You mean there was a plague in the United States?" a girl asked.

"All continents. It was finally halted by the

development of an antiserum which combated the bacillus responsible for the disease."

"I remember reading that the plague was caused by rat bites," a boy said.

"By rats and by bites, but not by rat bites," Mrs. Phelps explained. "Rats carry fleas and the fleas are the carriers of the bacillus. It is spread by the bite of the flea."

"Thank goodness we don't have rats running around any more," a girl said.

"That's a joke," James said. "My father's a fireman in New York City and he told me they figure there are more rats in New York than there are people."

"But we don't have the plague any more . . . right?" a girl asked.

"We don't have epidemics, but there are still over two thousand cases of the plague reported worldwide each year," Mrs. Phelps said.

"In some places in the world it still isn't much different from the Dark Ages," a boy said.

"You're right. For example, in some places they still practice agriculture in ways more connected to the sixteenth century than to modern western civilizations," Mrs. Phelps agreed. "But in spite of our up-to-date technology, there are still, right here in the United States, on average, twenty cases of the plague each year."

"And people die?" that same girl asked, sounding anxious.

"Very rarely. The mortality rate, if treatment is received quickly, is less than 1 percent," Mrs. Phelps said.

The girl looked relieved. Did she really think she was going to get the plague?

"Many diseases, such as smallpox, which caused great hardship around the world, have been eliminated completely," Mrs. Phelps continued. "The only smallpox virus in the world is kept in a few special, secure laboratories as a scientific curiosity."

"Will that happen to the plague some day?" James asked.

Mrs. Phelps shook her head. "Unlikely. There are literally millions of animals and billions of fleas on those animals that carry the plague bacillus."

That didn't sound so encouraging–especially if you thought about all those rats that were in New York.

"Plague bacillus is a natural occurrence, not unlike a hurricane or tornado or earthquake. We can't stop those, either."

"But even hurricanes and tornadoes and earthquakes are different for us, here in the States, than in some other places," James said.

"I'm not sure if I can agree with that. The midwest of our country is a hotbed for tornadoes, Florida and the Gulf Coast are often on hurricane alert, and the whole of California sits on the San

Andreas Fault and has experienced numerous earthquakes and–"

"I don't mean we don't *have* natural disasters," James said. "What I mean is that even though we have those we don't suffer the same way. I watch the news and hear about earthquakes happening in places like China and they have twenty thousand deaths, and when we have one in California there's only twenty people killed, maybe less."

"Maybe they have bigger earthquakes there," a girl said.

"I don't think so. The same strength of earthquake has different results in different places," James said.

"That's the same with hurricanes," I said, backing up what James was saying. "I remember hearing how thirty thousand people were killed by a hurricane in Bangladesh last year . . . or was it the year before . . . well, anyway, whenever it happened, there's usually only one or two people killed when there's a hurricane here."

"I'd never really thought of it, but you boys are right," Mrs. Phelps said. "And what are your names?"

"I'm James Bennett and this is my friend, Will Fuller."

Great, now she knew my name . . . but now that girl knew my name too. Not a bad trade-off.

"So, James and Will, why do you think that these naturally occurring phenomena don't create the same fatalities in this country as they do in other parts of the world?"

"It's the same as with the plague," James said.

"Can you explain that?"

"Sure. It's like the way modern medicine and drugs protect us from the plague. High-quality construction materials, building standards and early-warning systems for hurricanes and tornadoes reduce fatalities, at least here in places like the U.S. or Canada or France . . . you know . . . places that are more modern."

"That's very well explained, James," Mrs. Phelps said.

"Thanks. I did a project on this stuff last year," he said.

I didn't think I would have told her that. I would have just let her think that I was smart.

"While we still have these potential dangers, we have a level of protection that makes us feel more secure, almost immune," Mrs. Phelps said.

"Not immune," James pointed out, "just safer."

"Yes, of course you're right. You seem to have given this a lot of thought, James. Are you planning on becoming some sort of civil engineer?"

He shook his head. "I'm going to be a fireman . . . like my father."

"That's great. You know, if you went back a few hundred years it was almost a given that you became whatever your father was. If your father was a blacksmith then you became a blacksmith. If he ran a store you took over the store when he died."

"And girls became what their mothers were," a girl said. "Wives and mothers and household slaves and not much more."

"Thank goodness that part of history has changed," Mrs. Phelps said. "But that reminds me: tomorrow, you will all be participating in your co-op placements."

Because of some sort of reorganization at the school, the teachers were meeting all day, and they had to figure out what to do with the students. We were all going out with somebody–parents or relatives or friends–to shadow them while they did their work.

"I was wondering where people are going tomorrow," Mrs. Phelps said. "James, are you going with your father?"

"Definitely. He's taking me to his station, in downtown Manhattan."

"That could be very exciting," Mrs. Phelps said.

"Could be, but won't be," James answered. "Unfortunately, I have to stay at the station all day. I'm not allowed to go out on the truck on a call."

"Sounds like a safety precaution, like the ones that keep us safe from hurricanes. What are other people doing?"

"I'm going with my mother to spend a day in the Emergency department. She's a doctor," a girl said. I think her name was Sarah.

"That will be a great opportunity. Do you think *you* want to be a doctor?"

"My mother said she'd like me to be anything *except* a doctor."

"I guess she has her reasons, and tomorrow you'll have a chance to see what those reasons might be."

Other people piped up about what they would be doing. One guy was going to spend a day at a vet's office. Another person was going to sit in court all day–his father was a judge. And a couple of kids were going to spend the day in an elementary school class with their teacher parents. I thought that was a goofy thing to do. We'd all spent a lot of time in schools already, and if you didn't know what a teacher did for a living by now you probably weren't smart enough to be one.

"Anybody else want to share their plans?" Mrs. Phelps asked.

"I'm not going with either of my parents," my dream girl said. "I'm going to be spending my day with my big brother . . . he works for MTV."

"Your brother works for *MTV*?" James asked, as people gasped and sat up in their seats.

"He works in the control room," she said. "He mixes videos, but he also gets to meet celebrities and go to parties and lots of stuff."

"Will you get to meet anybody famous?" a girl asked.

"I don't know . . . maybe. My brother says that there are always famous people around the place."

There was a murmur of conversation as people tried to imagine who she might meet. I didn't want her to meet anybody. I already knew I was going to be competing with guys in grade ten and up so I definitely didn't need a rock star in the mix. But she had the best placement, no question.

"And Will, what will you be doing?" Mrs. Phelps asked.

She caught me off guard. "Um . . . I'll be going with my father . . . to his office."

"And what does your father do?"

"He works for a trading company." Boy, did that sound boring. "Like, an international trading company–money markets and stocks and all that stuff." I hoped I sounded like I knew what I was talking about. "He's one of the head guys," I added, trying to make it sound at least a little bit interesting. "And his office is in Manhattan."

"That sounds like an interesting experience," Mrs. Phelps said.

"I guess so," I said, sounding less positive than she did.

"Now, since you're going to be away tomorrow I'm going to give you a double reading assignment. I want all of chapters two, three and four read by Wednesday. All of you have a great day tomorrow. Who knows, it might be an experience that changes your entire life!"

CHAPTER

TWO

I scraped the last bit of food off my plate and shoveled it into my mouth.

"Would you like seconds?" my mother asked.

"Thanks, but no thanks."

"Okay, but watching you wolf that down, I got the feeling that you really liked it."

"I did. I love your lasagna."

"Thank you. I like making things you enjoy."

I did like her cooking, but that wasn't why I had eaten so quickly. I was in a rush to get to James's place–we had a practice scheduled.

"There's lots more if you want another piece."

"Maybe later, for a bedtime snack. Besides, shouldn't you save some for Dad?"

"There's plenty for him."

"I have to get going," I said as I got up and took my dishes to the counter.

"Where to?"

"James's."

"Could you help me clean up before you go?"

"Sure, no problem." I was in a rush, but it was faster to do it than argue about it.

While my mother scrubbed the lasagna pan I loaded my stuff into the dishwasher and then headed back to get the rest of the things off the table. My father's place was all set–dinner plate, side plate, glass, cutlery and napkin. All untouched.

"Do you want me to leave the place for Dad, or put it away?"

"I guess you can leave it." She sounded tired.

"When did he say he'd be home?" I asked.

"He'll be home at seven . . . unless he calls again."

In our house it was important to either be on time or call and say when you were going to be home. My mother was a fanatic about that.

"Do you have any homework tonight?"

"A few chapters to read for history. I'm going to bring my textbook with me and James and I will go over it tonight."

"Before or after you play music?"

"What makes you think we're going to play tonight?" I asked.

"Aren't you?"

"Well, yeah."

"Just make sure you do your homework first, that's all I'm asking," she said.

"There's no rush. I have tomorrow night, too."

"Oh, that's right, you're spending the day with your father."

"Yeah."

She furrowed her brow. "You don't sound very excited."

"Well . . . I guess it's better than going to school."

"It should be very interesting. I know your father has been looking forward to it."

"He has?"

"He's been talking a lot about it," she said.

I shrugged. "I haven't seen him enough this week to know what he's been talking about."

"This has been a busy week for him," my mother said.

"And how is that different from any other week?"

My mother didn't answer right away. "Your father isn't happy with the situation either. He would like to be able to spend more time with us."

It seemed pretty simple to me. If he wanted to spend more time with us he just had to leave his office. I knew he had an important job, and that meant a lot of responsibility . . . as well as a big paycheck. But money wasn't a big problem for us. If we'd needed the cash, Mom could have gone back to work after I started school, but she chose to stay home and put in time with her charities and volunteer work, so we couldn't be that hard up.

"There, all done," I said as I loaded the last of the dishes into the washer.

My mother pulled the lasagna pan out of the soapy water in the sink.

"You boys must be getting pretty good considering how much you've been practicing."

"We're getting better."

"It's very nice of Mr. and Mrs. Bennett to let you use their basement."

"Yep."

"And they don't mind?"

"Nope. Mrs. Bennett says as long as she can hear us playing she knows where we are and that we're not getting into any trouble."

"And Mr. Bennett?"

"I think he likes us being there. He even came downstairs and played with us the other night."

She smiled. "He did?"

"Yeah, he plays guitar. It's all old school . . . you know, like Led Zeppelin and the Stones and the Beatles, but he can really play. He's pretty cool for an old guy."

"Old guy? He's about the same age as your father and me."

"That's what I said, for an *old guy.*" I smiled. "Actually, he's still in pretty good shape, too. Sometimes he plays some hoops with us on the driveway and he can almost keep up."

"Being fit is part of his job," my mother said. "You can't have a fat, unfit fireman." She paused. "It's been a while since you and your father played basketball together."

"A long time."

"Maybe you could challenge him to a game this weekend," she suggested.

"What are the chances he'll even be home this weekend?"

"Well, I don't see any business trips scheduled," she said, taking a look at the calendar on the side of the fridge.

"Just because they aren't scheduled doesn't mean they don't happen."

My mother looked sad. "Things do come up." She put a hand on my shoulder. "It's not easy, and it's not what any of us would want. It's just the way it is sometimes. Your father would love nothing better than to play some basketball with you, or even go over to James's place and jam with you boys."

"Jam?"

"Play along . . . that is the word, isn't it . . . jam?"

"Yeah. You got the word right–it was the idea of Dad playing an instrument that kind of freaked me out there."

"It's been a lot of years, but I imagine he can still play the drums."

"Oh yeah, Dad told me he used to play the drums when he was my age."

"It's probably like riding a bike," my mother said. "I can still picture your father in his friend's garage, playing with his band."

"He was in a band?" That I didn't know.

"I don't think they ever had a name or played anywhere except the garage, but they considered themselves a band . . . just the way you boys do."

We'd only played in the basement so far, but we had big plans, and we almost had a name.

"I can just picture your father, pounding away on those drums, his hair halfway down his back and–"

"Dad had hair halfway down his back?" I asked in amazement.

I'd started letting my hair grow at the end of school last year, but I was keeping my mouth shut about it and expecting any day to hear my father tell me to get a haircut. Mine still wasn't quite to my shoulders. "Everybody had long hair then. Haven't you seen any pictures of him from those days?"

"Not that I can remember."

"Your father wasn't born old, you know."

Maybe not old, but at least in his late twenties. I couldn't picture him as a teenager, doing teenager things.

"Your father used to be a pretty cool dude back then."

"Okay . . ."

"And your mother was one hot little–"

"That's way too much information!" I said, putting my hands over my ears. "I gotta get going. I'll be home by nine."

"No later. Don't forget how early your father leaves for work in the morning. And call me if you're not going to be at James's. You know how I worry."

"I will. See you later."

CHAPTER THREE

It was barely light. I slumped down farther into the front seat of my dad's car, closing my eyes, trying to get at least a few minutes more sleep. I'd known my father hit the road early–he was usually gone long before I got up–but it was different *knowing* it and *doing* it. This might have been my father's usual morning, but it wasn't mine. And to make matters even worse I'd been up really late. After getting home from James's, I'd stayed up listening to tunes and putting together some lyrics for a song we were working on. I'd even picked up my history book and got a start on the reading assignment. It was after midnight by the time I turned out the light. Somehow I just couldn't make myself go to sleep any earlier than that. Now, I was paying the price. My father was full of energy and talking a mile a minute. Maybe he considered this "quality" parenting time. For me, there'd have been a lot more quality to it if he'd just shut up and let me sleep.

If you combined his early mornings with his late nights, business trips and the occasional work-filled weekend, there were times when it seemed like my father was more a rumor at our house than a confirmed fact. I once joked with James that if my parents ever got divorced, and didn't tell me about it, it would be weeks or even months before I figured it out. Not that he and my mom would ever get divorced. They still held hands, giggled together and always kissed goodbye and said, "I love you." At times it was almost a little bit sickening. I felt like yelling out, "You're married already so can you just knock it off?"

"Here we are," my father said as the car came to a stop.

I opened my eyes and climbed out. The sun was fully above the horizon now and I could see that the parking lot of the train station was almost completely filled. Apparently my father wasn't the only one who headed to a New York City office this early.

We climbed up the stairs and onto the platform. I followed my father as he wove his way through the crowd. He was easy to pick out because he was half a head taller than almost everybody else. He kept walking until we were at the far end of the platform. Strangely, it was almost deserted there.

"No crowd," I said.

"People all cluster around the entrance and then fight to get seats. Back here is the best place. I never have a problem."

"Then why don't other people come back here?" I asked.

"Humans are herd animals. We all like huddling together. It makes us feel safe and secure. In fact, one of the best ways to get ahead is to try to move in one direction while everybody else is moving in the other."

I looked at my father. "Aren't we moving in the same direction as everybody else . . . into the city?"

"We are, but *we* are going to be *sitting*. Here comes the train now."

I looked up the tracks. I could see the engine of the train, trailing behind a bright, bright headlight. It got bigger and bigger and brighter and brighter. I had to avert my eyes. The big engine surged down the tracks, a wave of sound and wind preceding it into the station.

"Step back a little," my father said as he put a hand across my chest.

That was stupid. I wasn't five years old any more and–a blast of wind blew my hair back as the train squealed into the station, slowed down and came to a stop. The big doors opened up right in front of us and we climbed up and into the train car.

"This way," my father said.

I followed behind him. He passed a number of open sets of seats and then gestured for me to sit down.

"No, no . . . take that one," my father said, pointing to the seat by the window. I shuffled over.

"This is where I always sit."

"Every day?"

"Every day I've gone to work for the past ten years."

Talk about being in a rut. I looked around the car. It was less than a quarter full. Some of the people were reading newspapers or books. Others were already working on their laptops, or had headphones clipped to their heads, lost in their music. A couple of people were dozing off. A few stared out the windows. What exactly did they find so fascinating? It certainly wasn't what I would call a scenic view–nothing but old cement embankments, backyards of houses and factories that had seen better and busier days.

The train slowed down as it came into the next station. As it came to a stop my father got to his feet.

"We don't get off here . . . do we?" I asked as I started to get to my feet as well.

"Not here. End of the line at Grand Central. We're not getting off but other people *are* getting on."

Of course people were getting on . . . but what did that have to do with him getting up? Was he giving up his seat? The doors opened and people came up the stairs.

"Good morning, John!" a man called out to my father as he walked up the aisle. They shook hands and the man plopped down into the window seat directly across from me. Then another man sat down beside me–taking my father's seat! At the same time a woman sat down opposite him, leaving my father no place to sit.

"Here you go," the woman said as she offered me a steaming cup.

I drew slightly back.

"It's coffee. Two creams and three sugars," she said.

My mouth dropped open. How could she possibly have known that was how I took my coffee?

"Isn't that the way you like it?" she asked. She looked up at my father. "You did tell me that was how he drank his coffee, right, John?"

I felt relieved. Obviously she knew my dad. I took the cup from her hand. She handed a second cup to my father.

"The important thing is that you got mine right," my father said.

"Black, plain, no nothing. Pretty boring."

That was how my father took his coffee. That was also how he was. He wore the same suit to work every day–actually, one of about a half-dozen black suits he had in the closet. When we'd bought our new car last year we'd simply got the newer version of our old Volvo station wagon. I had a pretty good idea what our *next* new car would be, too.

My dad wasn't much for change or trying new things. He liked the same foods. He was a real meat-and-potatoes sort of guy. We went to the same resort in Maine every year for holidays. There were hardly any surprises with my father.

"I'm tempted to get you something different one morning," the woman said. "I'm thinking a double espresso latte with a frosting of cinnamon. So, John, are you going to introduce us to your son?"

"Of course. Will, this wonderful woman is Vanessa, and these two fine gentlemen are Steve and Elliott."

I shook hands with all three.

"The four of us ride in together every morning," my father explained.

"Every morning?"

"Unless one of us is sick or on holiday," my father said.

"We share coffee and conversation," Steve added.

"And we take turns bringing the coffee," Vanessa said. "It isn't always me. I wouldn't want these three *males* to get the idea that it's a woman's job to bring the coffee."

"I'd never say anything like that," Elliott said, "especially not if my wife could hear . . . she'd kill me!"

Everybody laughed.

"Thanks for the coffee," I said.

"That's all right. For a split second I almost forgot to order it. Habit. But your father would have been upset with me. He's been talking about you joining us for the last week or so."

"That's practically *all* he talked about on the ride in yesterday," Steve said.

I suddenly felt a pang of guilt. I'd almost blown off the whole day by saying that I was feeling sick and just staying in bed. After he'd left for work, and there was no way I could get into the city and join him, I would have made a miraculous recovery and found something else to do. Maybe my father was looking forward to this, but I sure wasn't.

"Actually, I think Vanessa was even more excited than your father," Elliott said.

"And why shouldn't I be?" she demanded, pretending to be angry. "We've been hearing his dad tell us all about him for years and showing us all those pictures. I wanted to see if the real thing was as wonderful as his father always claimed he was."

She seemed pretty friendly. I wondered if Mom knew about Vanessa.

"And?" my father asked.

"He's even better looking than his pictures."

I felt myself start to blush.

"Forget being better looking than the pictures. He's much better looking than his *father*," Steve joked.

"Kid must get his looks from his mother," Elliott added.

"Actually, most people think he looks like me," my dad said.

"You?" Steve said. "I guess if you were looking at some sort of strange, funhouse, distorted-mirror version, then you'd look identical."

My grandparents said that I did look like my father when he was my age. From the pictures I'd seen I had to agree.

My father was tall and had broad shoulders. He looked like the ex-football player that he was, standing over six-four and weighing close to two hundred and forty pounds. I figured that some day I'd fill out too, because I was already pretty big for my age.

The four of them continued to banter and joke and kid each other. It was obvious from their quips and comments that they really did know, and like, each other.

"Hey, Will, are you a sports fan?" Elliott asked.

"I love sports."

"You follow the right teams? Or are you a loser like your old man?"

"Who are you calling a loser?" my father shot back.

"What else would you call somebody who cheers for the Jets, the Mets *and* the Rangers?"

"You don't know what you're talking about," my father protested. "The Jets are going to have a great season this year."

"They certainly didn't have a great *start* to their season," Elliott said. "What was the final score in that game . . . Colts 25, Jets 24?"

"They *almost* won," my father argued.

"'Almost won' is the way losers describe losing, and that's the whole story of the Jets."

"The Jets are going to be winners by the end. This is the year they're going all the way."

"The only way that's going to happen is if Broadway Joe Namath comes out of retirement . . . after he invents a time machine," Steve said and began laughing.

"And didn't the Mets lose again last game, too?" Elliott asked.

"To the Florida Marlins," my father admitted.

"While our beloved New York Yankees pummeled the Red Sox 7 to 2. Now, the Yankees, that's a team that's going all the way."

"You figure they're going to win the Super Bowl?" my father joked.

"They have about as much chance as the Jets do," Steve said. "Isn't it about time you started cheering for a real team . . . like the Yankees?"

"I do cheer for the Yankees," my father said. "I cheer for them to lose. Cheering for the Yankees to win is like getting up at six in the morning in the dark and cheering for the sun to rise. What's the challenge?"

"So you admit that the Yankees are going to take the World Series?" Steve said, pouncing on his words.

"I admit that they probably will win, with all the money they spend, but I'm hoping they don't."

"So, Will, who do you cheer for?" Steve asked.

"Rangers, Jets and Mets," I said, and my father laughed and gave me a little punch on the shoulder.

"Okay, now I *am* seeing the resemblance between you two," Steve said.

The train started to slow down again.

"We'll have to finish this discussion later," my father said.

"It was a pleasure to meet you," Vanessa said as she, and then Steve and Elliott, shook my hand, stood up and started toward the door.

I started to follow after them when my father grabbed my arm. "They're heading in a different direction for a different subway."

My father walked the length of the car and into the next one. He eased his way through the crowd that was gathering at each door. We went through a second car, then a third and fourth and finally joined a line waiting to exit. Almost on cue the train stopped and the door popped open. We shuffled down and directly into an exit that was right outside the door.

"After doing this for years you figure out which doors open where and all the little shortcuts to make the day faster and easier," he said as we hurried down the steps that led from the platform.

I felt a little anxious being caught in the push and shove of the crowd. Everybody seemed to be in some sort of race—a race where everybody was wearing a suit and tie and carrying a briefcase or a bag. It was hard not to be drawn into the rush, into the excitement. And why not? This wasn't just any place. We were in New York City. In the heart of New York City, the center of the country . . . heck, the center of the universe. And here we were just a short subway ride away from the very heart of the heart . . . where my father's office was . . . the World Trade Center.

CHAPTER

FOUR

We came up from the subway and onto the street. I was going to ask how far we had to walk when I looked up and saw the World Trade Center towers looming above my head. They dominated the sky–the two most impressive buildings in the most impressive skyline in the entire world.

"Pretty amazing, isn't it?" my father said as we walked along.

"Yeah, no question."

We were part of a crowd of people moving along the sidewalk, a river of humanity, flowing around street vendors and fire hydrants and signs that were like rocks in the stream. On the crowded streets the cars–every second one a yellow cab–bumped along. We were actually moving a little faster than they were. I didn't know why people didn't just get out of their cabs and walk. It was a beautiful day, already warm and probably on the way to being hot. The sky was so blue, without a trace of a single cloud, that it looked like something from a postcard. It felt more like a summer day than a September day. It was a nice day not to be in school. Then again, being in my father's office wouldn't be that much different or better. Maybe I should have gone with my first plan and told him I was sick. Then I could have just hung out and had the day to myself.

We walked across the plaza and stopped right in front of the twin buildings. I let my eyes follow up, up, up, until I was practically leaning over backwards to capture the very tops of the towers. They stretched up to the sky in a series of thin, parallel lines–two glowing, golden towers reflecting the morning light. The Twin Towers. They looked so impressive against the brilliant blue sky.

"I've been working here for almost twelve years and I still sometimes just stand here and stare," my father said.

"I can understand why."

"When they were first built, some people complained about how ugly they were. They had interviews with architects saying that they were unimaginative, boring, that they proved the bankruptcy of American design. I think they actually show the imagination that this country is built on. They are big, impressive, and represent the boundless energy that makes this country great. They are beautiful. They symbolize New York, the same way the Eiffel Tower *is* Paris, or the pyramids *are* Egypt, or Big Ben *is* London. These towers *are* New York. Big, bold, clean lines stretching up into a limitless sky. If New York is the center of the universe–and really, who could dispute that?–then these two towers are the center of the *center*."

"You won't get any argument from me."

"You know, there are actually *seven* buildings in the Trade Center complex. The two towers, of course, are the ones everybody knows. The North Tower was completed in 1971 and the South Tower was finished in 1974."

"How tall are they?"

"Just over 1360 feet, 110 stories. Of course the North Tower also has an aerial that rises another 300 feet. Come on, let's go in."

We walked over to the side of the South Tower and entered through a really unimpressive little door. Instantly we were in what looked more like a shopping mall than the foot of the World Trade Center. There were dozens and dozens of stores, all open and apparently doing big business. They were crowded–the whole mall was crowded.

People were everywhere, rushing around in all directions.

A double set of escalators led up from underneath. They were packed with people, two by two, marching out of the ground like little ants. There were two other empty escalators leading down. Above both were signs indicating that below were trains and buses and a subway station. I wondered why we hadn't taken that subway to get here, but I didn't ask.

We joined in a long line of people taking a second set of escalators. We came off at the top and were deposited right into the lobby of the building. This was more like it. High, high ceilings, soaring thirty or forty feet above our heads. Red carpets beneath our feet and large slabs of beautiful, gleaming white marble and gigantic floor-to-ceiling windows letting in the brilliant sunshine. This looked like the entrance to some sort of museum or a fancy palace. Looking around, I realized I was the only person who seemed impressed. All around us people continued to rush by, busy and bustling, carrying briefcases, cellphones held to their ears, completely ignoring their surroundings and each other. I guess for them it was just another day at work.

"I'm going to tell you some of what you'd get from a guided tour," my father said.

I was sure before he started that he knew everything there was to know about these towers. On a shelf in our den were a dozen books about the World Trade Center. My father didn't just work here, he was fascinated by the place. He could probably have told me more facts about his office building than about our own house. Then again, he spent more time here than he did at home.

"These towers have a unique design," he began. "The outer walls are a rigid series of hollow tubes spaced twenty-two inches apart, linking through floor trusses to a central core to provide the strength and flexibility needed for a building this size. While it soars over thirteen hundred feet up, it also goes down over seventy feet. They excavated until they hit solid bedrock. Each tower has 21,800 windows and 104 passenger elevators, and the total cost of construction was slightly over 1.5 *billion* dollars."

"That's an awful lot of money," I said, trying to act interested.

"In today's dollars that would be well over 2 billion. Come on, let's go up."

We walked along into the central core. There were banks and banks of elevators–I guess 104 elevators, although it didn't look like there could possibly be that many. In front of each elevator was a line of people waiting to go up. Over top of each door was a bank of lights flashing from one floor to another as the elevators raced up or down the tower.

"Each elevator is super-fast and is meant to carry fifty-five people. No elevator goes to every floor. There's a combination of local and express elevators. From the lobby there are elevators that serve eight-floor sections of the tower, all the way up to the forty-fourth floor. There are some elevators that go express right to the forty-fourth floor, where there is a sky lobby. From there, more local elevators serve the next thirty-four floors right up to floor seventy-eight, where there is another sky lobby for transfer to elevators that go up to the top. There are also some elevators in the lobby that go, express, right to the sky lobby on the seventy-eighth floor."

"How do you know which elevator goes where?"

"Look above the door and it shows what floors are served by that elevator. It's simple, really."

"Wouldn't it be simpler if they all just stopped at every floor all the way to the top?" I asked.

"That was one of the engineering issues they had to address. To do that, the whole building would be nothing but elevators with no space left for offices. This way they can stagger the elevators and still get everybody to their office. You have to remember that each tower houses a small city of people, around twenty thousand workers in each one. I still find that number amazing. My whole town had only five hundred people."

My father had grown up in a little hick town in upstate New York.

"Just think, you could fit forty towns as big as mine in this one building!"

"That's a lot of people . . . but don't any of the elevators go all the way to the top?" I asked.

"Just one, and it doesn't make any stops along the way. It's the express elevator to the Observation Deck on the 107th floor. That's the one we're going to take."

"We're going to the Observation Deck?"

"I thought that would be a good place to start the day, looking out on the greatest city in the world!"

I followed my father to the express elevator. It had a much shorter line than the others. The elevator pinged and the door opened to reveal an empty car. We shuffled forward along with the crowd until we were swallowed up by the car. The door closed and almost instantly the car started moving.

I hated heights and I hated small spaces. Elevators were pretty much the worst combination of those two things I could imagine. The ride was so smooth that I hardly had any sense of speed or movement, but I still knew it was happening.

I tried to get my mind off of the elevator. Instead, I looked around at the people sharing the ride. They all avoided eye contact. They were almost all dressed in business suits. None of them looked the least bit like tourists, but they couldn't all work on the Observation Deck, could they?

The elevator started to slow down while my stomach continued to rise at the same speed. I felt myself rise slightly up out of my shoes before the ride settled to a stop. The door opened and the people raced off, sweeping us along with them.

"Welcome to the Observation Deck," my father said.

We walked away from the elevator and toward the glass. Stretched out before us was the city, and beyond that the Statue of Liberty sitting on an island, surrounded by glistening green water. Farther over was Staten Island and then the ocean. What an incredible sight!

My father thought the World Trade Center was what represented America, but for me it was the Statue of Liberty. Maybe new people didn't come to our country by boat any more, but that statue was what we were about. What did it say? "Give me your poor, your tired, your huddled masses . . ." Looking out over the city it was obvious that while the *huddled* part still fit, there were no *poor* to be seen from where I stood. Everywhere I looked was money, money and more money. Maybe my father was right and the World Trade Center and all the money that passed through here each day really did represent the United States.

I was amazed by how much green I could see interspersed with the buildings and streets. Aside from Central Park there were dozens and dozens of other little parks, patches of green among the gray and black. I really hadn't expected that.

"On a clear day, like today, you can see for forty-five miles," my father said.

"So, technically, we could see our house from here."

"We could, if we were looking in the right direction. We have to go to the other side."

I trailed behind him, keeping an eye out through the glass but also keeping a healthy distance away from the window. I'd have enjoyed the view a lot more from lower down–if that made any sense at all.

I noticed that we were practically the only people on the Observation Deck. What had happened to the people we rode up with?

"Where did everybody else go to?" I asked.

"They're at work on the floors below us. Some people take the express elevator to the top and then walk down the stairs to their offices."

"Why would they do that?" I asked.

"To save time. Time is money. Depending on the crowds waiting at the bottom it's often faster to simply take the express elevator to the top and walk down the stairs. Some people do the same at the end of the day, walking up the stairs to take the elevator down."

"Do you ever do that?" I asked.

He laughed. "My office is on the eighty-fifth floor. That's twenty-two floors down . . . or, more to the point, twenty-two floors *up* that I'd have to climb."

"That would take a long time."

"It would. I do take the stairs a lot, though. If I have to go five or even ten floors down or three or four stories up I'll hit the stairs. I find it saves time. I hate waiting for elevators. Actually, I hate waiting for anything."

My father stopped walking. "Our house is that way," he said, pointing into the distance.

I squinted in the bright sunshine, straining to see. My attention was caught by some motion off to the side. There was a small airplane flying along the river and I was looking *down* at it. I was actually watching a plane in flight from above it. That was beyond belief. I was so high up that planes were flying *below* me!

"Do you remember the last time you were up here?" my father asked.

"Not really."

"You were only four or five at the time. You know, that's typical of us New Yorkers. Here we are in a city that draws hundreds of millions of people from around the world and we don't take advantage of the amazing things that are all around us. The Empire State Building, Greenwich Village, the United Nations building, Radio City Music Hall, Times Square, Broadway, the Statue of Liberty–when was the last time you saw the Statue of Liberty?"

"Just now, out the window," I said, pointing to the other side of the building.

"I meant up close, on the island."

"I'm not sure, but it was a long time ago."

"We have to go there some time soon. We should become visitors in our own city. This should just be the start of our sight-seeing tour of New York!"

I wasn't sure how I felt about that. Did I really want to see any of those sights? But then again, what did it matter? The way my father worked I'd have to wait until he retired before he really did take me anywhere. Lots of talk didn't mean much. Work would always be more important than anything–or anybody–else.

"Close your eyes," my father said.

"What?"

"Close your eyes."

Reluctantly I did what he'd requested, although I sure didn't know why.

"Can you feel it?" he asked.

"Feel what?"

"The building sway."

I opened up my eyes. "What?"

"The tower. It moves. On a windy day it can sway three feet away from center. Now stand very still, don't move, don't talk, just close your eyes and see if you can feel it."

I closed my eyes again. I didn't feel anything. Just my feet on the carpeting and–wait a second–I could feel something. There was a gentle, ever-so-slight movement.

"Well?" he asked.

I opened my eyes and nodded my head.

"Today the winds are light, but on a very windy day you can *really* feel it. Now imagine a tightrope stretched between this tower and the other."

I looked over at the North Tower.

"A man actually walked between the two buildings. Can you picture that?"

Enough that it made my knees get all weak and gooey just thinking about it.

"People have also parachuted off the top of the North Tower."

"They let people parachute from the building?" I asked in amazement.

He shook his head. "Nobody let them. They broke in through the doors at the top to get to the roof. They call them base jumpers, and jumping from the World Trade Center is supposed to be one of the ultimate thrills. You ever wonder if you might want to try skydiving?"

"I don't think so." I wouldn't do that for a million dollars.

"There was also some man who used specially designed suction cups to climb up the side of the building. I was at work at the time but he didn't pass by my office window. That would have been strange, working at your desk, turning around and there, plastered against the glass, a man silhouetted against the city."

"That is just too bizarre. Why would somebody risk his life doing something like that?"

"People are willing to risk their lives for all sorts of reasons, some of which I'll never understand. Probably the strangest thing I've ever seen while working here was when they were filming the remake of the movie *King Kong*. Try to visualize gigantic Styrofoam and inflatable monkey parts clinging to the side of the building."

"That would be weird. They film lots of movies here, don't they?"

"Here and around here. These towers are in countless movies." My father looked at his watch. "We'd better get going. The day is almost half over."

"Half over? It's not even eight-thirty yet."

"Eight-thirty here, but after twelve in London and Paris. We do a great deal of our business in those two cities. That's why I always try to arrive so early."

"That makes sense," I said. I thought for a second. "But then those cities should close early, which means you could come home early, right?"

"Well . . . then we have to connect with the Los Angeles market, which is three hours later."

"Good thing you don't do business in Japan, I guess."

"Oh, we do!"

"Then maybe you should just sleep here and save yourself the commute home," I said sarcastically.

"Actually, we have two staff who stay here at night to monitor the Asian market. The sun never sets on the business empire, and money never sleeps. Now we'd better get to the elevators. We have to take the express down to the lobby, catch one there for the seventy-eighth floor and then a local up to the eighty-fifth, where I work." He looked at his watch. "It's going to be a long wait at this time of day in the main lobby. And from the seventy-eighth floor we could just walk up seven flights . . . I do that some of the time."

"Wouldn't it be easier to just walk down from here?"

"That's twenty-two floors."

"Twenty-two floors *down*. That wouldn't take nearly as long as going all the way down and back up again, would it?"

He nodded his head. "I think it would probably save some time . . . and frustration. I hate just standing there and waiting."

"Me too," I said, although a big part of it for me was that I didn't want to climb into any more elevators.

"Sounds good. Let's take the stairs."

CHAPTER FIVE

My father led us toward the stairwell, right beside the elevator. I was glad to get away from the windows. The view was nice, but nicer from a little bit farther back.

Somehow I'd expected the stairwell of the World Trade Center to be fancier or different in some way. It was just plain concrete stairs, metal railings, nine steps between landings, eighteen steps between floors. The sound of our footsteps echoed off the walls as we walked.

"You know what's always struck me as stupid?" my father said.

"What?"

"Half the people who work here belong to fitness centers. They leave the office, jump in their cars or taxis and travel halfway across town to go and climb on a Stairmaster, when all they had to do was simply take the stairs instead of the elevator when they got to the office in the first place."

"You said you take the stairs sometimes."

"Sometimes, but not as often as I should. I like that it's quiet and private. Just think, there's a small city of people in this building and we're the only ones in this stairwell for probably thirty floors."

We continued down, floor by floor. I started trying to do the math in my head. There were 18 steps per floor and we were going down 22 floors. If there were 20 steps in each floor then that would be 440 . . . minus 22 multiplied by 2 . . . that would make 396 steps.

Now how many steps would it be to get up to the eighty-fifth floor if we were coming from the lobby? That would be 85 multiplied by 18, or I guess 84 because you started at floor 1 so you only had to climb 84 floors. But the lobby was at least three stories tall, so the second floor might actually be the fourth floor. And did this building have a thirteenth floor, or was the thirteenth marked as the fourteenth because of superstition or–?

"Here we are," my father said.

In large black numerals on the back of the door it said "85." He opened it and motioned for me to go through. Instantly we were standing in an office. There were desks separated by partitions, computers, ringing phones, people sitting and standing and rushing around. It looked busy, almost frantic. The stairwell really was a quiet little oasis compared to this.

"This is it . . . this is my office."

"John!" a woman called out as she rushed over. "It's after eight-thirty and you weren't here! I was ready to start checking the hospitals or the morgue. You're never late. You got us all worried. Just where have you been?"

"I've was up on the Observation Deck."

"The *what*?" she asked, sounding as shocked as if he'd just told her he'd been on an alien spaceship.

"The Observation Deck . . . with my son."

"Your son . . . oh, that's right. This is your day to bring him with you." She looked at me. "So this is William."

"Will," I said.

"And Will, this charming but frantic woman is not an escaped psychiatric patient but my colleague, Suzie," my father said.

"Pleased to meet you," she said as she reached out, grabbed my hand and pumped my arm up and down.

"I'm pleased to meet you, too." She was younger than my dad, small and blond and . . . well, kind of cute.

"And just for the record, you practically *have* to be a psychiatric patient to work here," she said.

"Then Suzie must be truly crazy because she's been my personal assistant for almost nine years."

"Personal assistant," she said, shaking her head. "That means secretary. I'm your father's secretary."

"You do a whole lot of things that go well beyond the role of secretary," my father said.

"Yeah? Then how about paying me more instead of just giving me a fancy title?" she demanded, putting on a show of being angry.

"Suzie, if it were up to me you'd be the third-highest-paid person in the whole company, right after the president and, of course, me."

"Yeah, like that's going to happen. Now how about if you get to work so we can make this company a few million dollars and maybe, just maybe, some of it will find its way into my pay? You've already got three messages from London and you have a conference call with Paris in," she looked at her watch, "in less than five minutes, and you haven't even looked at the report."

"Damn, I forgot about that call. Thanks for reminding me."

"No problem. That's just part of the job of a secre– I mean, a personal assistant."

"Could you take care of Will, show him around the place, and I'll have a look at that report?"

"No problem. Just get going."

"Will, is that okay with you?" my father asked.

"Sure."

So much for him spending the day with me. I'd expected him to pawn me off on somebody at some point. I just hadn't expected it to happen within the first two minutes of hitting his office.

My father gave me a pat on the back like I was a five-year-old and then rushed off across the office. He had gone no more than a dozen steps when he was practically assaulted by a couple of women asking questions, and one of them shoved a report into his hands. They trailed after him and all three disappeared into his office.

"This place couldn't function without your father," Suzie said.

"We've sort of gotten used to it at home," I said, sarcastically.

"He does put in long hours," she said. "I can't even count the number of times he's tried to leave early to get home for a family meal or for something special–you certainly play a lot of school sports, don't you?"

"Yeah," I said, surprised that she knew that.

"It sounds like you were on practically every team in your last school."

"All of them," I said.

She nodded. "Your father's always bragging about you."

I shrugged, not knowing what to say about that. "I guess it's going to be harder at high school, with more competition," I finally said.

"From the way your father talks about you, I don't think you'll have too much trouble. He was always trying to sneak out to catch one of those games, and then one of our accounts would blow up, or somebody would grab him to talk about something and he just couldn't get out. Like I said, I can't even count the times that's happened."

Maybe I couldn't have counted the times he'd *tried*, but I could easily have counted the times he'd actually shown up. I could have counted them on the fingers of one hand without even using the thumb.

I didn't want to talk about that. It just got me annoyed. "Why do you have so many televisions?" I asked instead, pointing to a bank of ten sets mounted up on the wall, almost at the ceiling.

"Those are satellite-relayed stations from around the world. Each one shows the financial news from a country where we do business. That one in the corner is from France, and the one beside it is Italy . . . and then there's Germany and Japan and Russia, and three are from right here in the States."

"That one in the center is CNN, isn't it?" I asked.

"Yes, that's CNN. We watch it for breaking news."

I looked more closely at the pictures. Each one was different, but there were a whole lot of similar features. Everybody sat behind a desk and was wearing a suit, and there was a crawl of information along the bottom of each screen. On some of the screens the words were in languages I didn't understand, and some didn't even look like words, but symbols or squiggles.

"We need to know what's happening as close to the time it happens as possible," Suzie explained.

"Isn't that hard with the sound turned off?"

"The sound is off here, but each set is being monitored by at least one person who is responsible for that zone."

"People get paid to watch TV?" I asked in amazement. That sounded like my dream job.

"A few minutes could make the difference of tens or even hundreds of thousands of dollars in profit."

"That's a lot of money."

"It's all relative. We have to know what's happening everywhere because everywhere is connected to everywhere else. An oil tanker crashes in the Suez Canal and oil prices rise. An early frost in Florida hits the citrus industry and the price of orange juice rises. The central bank in Italy raises the interest rate and the price of the euro dips."

I didn't see how any of that could work.

"The world is a very small place. We are all connected as business and technology bring us all together."

I guess I couldn't really argue with that. I looked around the office "How many people work here?"

"This branch has just over a hundred people, while worldwide our company has more than twenty-five hundred employees."

"That's pretty big."

"And your father is one of the biggest guys. He's the senior VP in this office, which makes him one of the most important people."

"Most important in this office?"

"Most important in the world. In this office he's officially number two, but with the president away so much your father is often in charge, like he is today."

"I guess I knew he was important. I'm still not sure, though, what it is that he's in charge *of.* I know what you do here . . . sort of," I confessed.

"It's pretty simple. Just think of this as a really big store, kind of a version of the store at the corner of your street. But instead of individual customers we have companies that do business. Instead of dealing in hundreds of dollars we deal in hundreds of thousands and millions of dollars. Instead of people walking in with cash and out with goods, all our transactions are electronic. Instead of serving a neighborhood we serve the whole globe. And here we don't just sell, we also buy. Sometimes people walk in and sell us things. So instead of a store, it's maybe more like a pawnshop. In any case, it all involves sales and money. We try to buy low and sell high. That's how we make a profit. Does that make sense?"

"I guess so, but–"

"Suzie!" a man said excitedly as he rushed over. "I need to see the boss. Does he have any time this morning?"

"Probably not. He's dealing with a very important client. This gentleman right here," she said, pointing at me.

"Client?" he questioned, looking at me in a confused way.

"Yes, he's the founder of a dot-com company. He's the youngest billionaire in the United States."

"I . . . I didn't know . . . I'm pleased to–"

"Phil, I'm joking. This is John's son, Will," Suzie said and started laughing.

"John's son?" Phil said. "In that case I'm even *more* pleased to meet you." He reached out and pumped my hand enthusiastically.

"I've known your old man for a long time," Phil said. "He's a hell of a good guy. You must be very proud of him."

"Sure . . . yeah . . . I guess," I mumbled. "Proud" wasn't usually a word that came to mind when I thought about my father.

"Your dad is the glue that keeps this office together. Without him the place wouldn't be able to function. I wouldn't even want to think about how many jobs he saved during the last downturn. I'll catch up with your father later. You have yourself a great day!"

"Thanks." I couldn't help but wonder if people were saying these things because he was their boss or–

"Hang around here long enough and you're going to hear a lot of people talking about your dad that way," Suzie said in answer to my unspoken thought. "He really is very well respected and liked. That's a hard combination for a boss to be–both respected *and* liked–but your dad manages it. Come on."

I followed her across the office. I was amazed how noisy and chaotic it seemed. How did anybody get anything done with all of this going on? We stopped in front of a partially closed door–the brass plate indicated that it was my father's office. Suzie pushed the door open. My father was leaning back in his chair, feet up on his desk. He smiled and motioned for us to come in.

His office was big, and one wall was lined with a gigantic bookshelf. There were pictures of me and Mom on one of the shelves. There was a couch, and two big, comfy-looking leather seats, and his desk was a polished, reddish wood . . . not that I could see the top of the desk, it was covered in files and papers.

"The figures are clear. We need to be buying until it hits ninety-five," a voice said through the speaker phone on my father's desk.

"I think ninety-five is too optimistic," another voice said. "My projections take into account factors that may result in sales peaking lower. Ninety-five doesn't give us enough margin for error."

"What are you suggesting?" my father asked.

"Ninety-four."

"Ninety-four is being too cautious," the first voice said.

"Better cautious than careless," the second voice countered.

"I'm not just guessing, you know. I'm confident that the ceiling is at least ninety-five and more likely a point higher than that."

"I don't agree with what–"

"Gentlemen," my father said, cutting him off. "You have both stated your views–well thought out and backed by sound figures and reasoning–but now it's time to make a decision. It's time for *me* to make a decision." He paused and took a sip from his ever-present can of Coke. My father honestly believed Coke was a breakfast drink.

"I have immense respect for both of you gentlemen. You are two of the best in the business."

"Thank you," one of the voices said.

"I'd have to agree," said the second, and all three men laughed.

I looked past my father and out his window–or I guess, really, windows. The windows in the building were only about two feet wide in any of the offices, bordered by the columns that held the building up. Through the windows I could see the North Tower over to the left. Behind it, and the rest of the open view, was of all of Manhattan. I could see the East River, the George Washington Bridge and, in the distance, JFK Airport. I looked closely and saw a tiny plane lift off. This was really an incredible view.

"I can't argue with either of your positions," my father said. "And I believe I would be seriously tempting fate to disagree with either of you. As such, I'm going to go for a position in the middle. We're going to buy until it hits ninety-four and a half. A compromise. Does that sound reasonable?"

"No argument here," one of the voices said.

"Or here," agreed the second.

"Good. Then please pass on those instructions to your traders. Take care, gentlemen, and we'll talk soon."

My father clicked a button on the phone and it went silent.

"That should work," my father said to Suzie.

"You'll keep them both happy without risking too much either way."

"The middle of the road isn't just for yellow lines and road kill," my father said, now turning to me. "It's usually the safest way to make a healthy profit while minimizing the risk. Does that make sense?"

"I guess so," I admitted. "But it seems like there isn't much difference between ninety-four, ninety-four and a half and ninety-five cents."

Suzie giggled. "Those aren't cents, those are dollars, so that's a fifty-cent difference, per share, and we're talking about a transaction involving over ten million shares. So that means a difference of about–"

"Five million dollars," I said, cutting her off. I was always good with numbers, like my father. "I guess that is a big difference. And what happens if you guess wrong?"

"The buck stops here," my father said, tapping his finger against the desk. "I've been lucky that most of the time I guess right."

"I don't think luck has much to do with it," Suzie said.

"Luck is a big part of–"

There was a thunderous explosion and my eyes widened as a brilliant flash of light burst outside the windows.

CHAPTER

SIX

I jumped backwards, bumping into Suzie, practically knocking her over. My father sprang out of his chair and jumped away from the window, nearly landing on his desk. The flash of light was gone. Outside the windows everything looked normal. We could see the North Tower right in front of us and the city stretching out beyond it.

"What was that . . . what happened?" Suzie gasped.

"There was an explosion of some sort and–"

"It's . . . it's snowing," I said, pointing out the window. Unbelievably, inexplicably, it was snowing!

"Maybe that was lightning," my father said, "and it produced some sort of freak snowstorm."

It was a virtual blizzard of big, white, fluffy flakes that were blowing in the gap between the two towers. I stared at it, transfixed, not able to believe my eyes . . . but why were some of the snowflakes glowing red? It looked as though their edges were on fire . . . but snow couldn't burn . . . could it?

"It's paper!" my father yelled. "Thousands and thousands of pieces of paper, and they're on fire!" He walked to the window. "Oh my God," he said.

I stumbled over until I stood right beside him. There, just above us, the entire side of the North Tower was a gaping hole! Smashed windows, jagged edges and flames, thick black smoke billowing up while pieces of paper blew out and fluttered down. I blinked my eyes, I rubbed them, trying to understand, trying to comprehend what I was seeing. I opened my eyes again. It was still there. This couldn't be real. I looked over at my father. His look of complete surprise, complete shock, mirrored my feelings and thoughts.

"What happened?" screamed out a voice from behind us.

I spun around. It was Phil. He and a half-dozen others spilled into the office. They looked worried, scared and confused–all of the things I was feeling.

"There's been an explosion in the North Tower," my father said. His voice was incredibly calm. "Almost at the top . . . around the ninetieth floor."

Everybody rushed forward to the window, pressing me forward, much closer to the windows than I ever would have gone on my own. My whole body shuddered and my knees were giving out. My heart was pounding so hard it felt like it was almost visible through my chest. I tried to shift away from the glass but couldn't move against or through the crush of bodies.

"What sort of explosion?" somebody asked.

"Could have been a lightning strike," Suzie said, echoing what my father had said when he thought it was snowing.

"Can't be," somebody answered. "The whole building is designed to absorb and redirect lightning. These towers get struck all the time with no damage."

"Besides, there's not a cloud in the sky," another man said. "Lightning has to come out of somewhere."

"Maybe it was a natural gas explosion," another woman suggested.

"Nope. No natural gas in the buildings."

"They could have been storing something flammable and it exploded."

"On the top floors of the World Trade Center?" a voice asked, incredulously. "At the prices they charge for floor space in these buildings there's no way anybody was using them for storage."

"Do you think it could be a bomb?" Phil asked.

A bomb? I figured that was just insane. But his question remained unanswered as nobody said a word. Did that silence mean that it *wasn't* such a crazy thought?

"Let's not go rushing to any conclusions," my father cautioned. "It could have been caused by a lot of things. Perhaps it was electrical, some sort of power surge or–"

"It was an airplane!" called out a voice from behind. We all spun around. "It was an airplane that hit the building. It's on CNN."

People abandoned the window and rushed out of the office toward the bank of TV sets. I trailed behind.

Up at ceiling level most of the screens were still showing the same talking heads–except for one. There, on the screen, was the building outside our window. There was black smoke billowing up and out of a gigantic gash . . . an ugly, raw hole that had erupted in the smooth glass skin of the building.

The camera panned around the tower. The footage was being shot from an airplane–no, a helicopter, hovering, circling around the building. A man reached and turned up the volume on the set.

"This is just in . . . I can hardly believe my eyes," the unseen announcer said. "While we have few details at this time I can tell you what little we do know. Just moments ago, at 8:46 a.m., a plane crashed into the North Tower, Building One, of the World Trade Center. It appears that it hit around the ninety-fourth floor. I repeat, an airplane has crashed into the North Tower of the World Trade Center. At this time, and we are in the process of receiving updates, we do not know the size of the plane, nor do we know the reasons for the crash, whether it was a result of pilot error or equipment failure or deliberate."

Deliberate? Why would a pilot deliberately crash a plane? It would be like suicide . . . wow . . . a public, spectacular suicide for the whole world to see.

"Got to be an accident," somebody said. "You know how people are always buzzing around the buildings on those tours of New York, showing off the city for tourists. Just a matter of time, I guess . . . I'm surprised it hasn't happened before this."

Suddenly a second television screen flashed over to the same scene. Then another picture, then another and another, until there was a whole bank of TV sets, almost all of them showing the same thing. Funny, all the pictures were the same, but some of them were slightly out of sync. Then I realized why. These shots were being beamed to countries around the world and then bounced back here. This was being seen, *live*, by people around the world! How unbelievably strange.

Even stranger, this was all happening right outside our building, visible through the windows, but we were all in here, huddled around the TVs rather than witnessing it with our own eyes. Maybe it was because seeing it on the screen, validated by the unseen announcer at CNN, made it more real.

No, that wasn't it. Here, watching the screen, it was safe and sanitary. Looking through the window, with our own eyes, unshielded by the lens of the camera and the thick glass of the screens, it was too dangerous to look at, like staring up at the sun. By watching it on TV we felt removed, distant, and that distance gave us protection.

"At this time," the announcer continued, "we have no word on fatalities."

That's right, there had to be injuries . . . deaths. The pilot of the plane, passengers, anybody who had been right there by the windows . . . the way *we* were right by the windows. That could have been us, a few floors lower and one building over. A shudder went through my body.

The screen was now split into two parts. On the left side was the image of the building. On the right was an announcer. Suit and tie, perfect hair and teeth.

"It would be expected that, aside from the plane's pilot and any passengers aboard, there will be fatalities in the building from the initial crash and then the subsequent fire. It is reported that the plane crashed into the north side of the North Tower."

"That can't be right," Phil said. "We can only see the *south* side of the tower. It had to have hit the south side. It must have just buzzed by our building."

"Maybe what we're looking at is where the plane came *out* of the building," Suzie suggested grimly.

"No way, that isn't possible. There's no way a little plane could pass right through the whole–"

"I'm just receiving an update," the announcer said, and Phil stopped. The announcer placed a hand against his ear. He was probably getting the information through his earpiece. "There is new information . . . it is now confirmed that the airplane that crashed into the North Tower of the World Trade Center was a commercial airplane."

There were gasps. This was now even more unbelievable, but Suzie was right. We weren't looking at the place where the plane had crashed into the tower, this was where it had crashed through the other side.

"While it is too early to know the exact number of fatalities in the building or on the plane, it can only be assumed that all passengers have perished. I repeat, it is assumed that all passengers aboard the plane have perished."

I heard whimpering and turned around, away from the TV. There were two women, both crying, with their arms around each other. A third woman was crying just behind them and there was a man beside her, working hard to force back the tears that I could see in his eyes.

Everybody else was solemn and silent. Aside from the announcer, the only other sound was the constant buzzing of telephones, left unattended and unanswered as everybody stood transfixed, frozen in place.

The image on some of the screens suddenly changed. It showed fire trucks, police cars and ambulances all parked haphazardly on the plaza at the foot of the buildings. All around them were emergency personnel, rushing into the building and escorting people out. I thought about that mass of people who'd been in the lobby of our building this morning. There had to be just as many people in that building as there were in this one, and they all had to get *out* of there.

"How many people work in that tower?" I asked.

"There are forty thousand in the two towers, so I'd imagine around twenty thousand," Suzie said.

That was right, that was what my father had mentioned this morning.

"Yeah, but there wouldn't be that many people there right now," Phil said. "It's still early."

"And a Tuesday," somebody else added. "People arrive late on Mondays and Tuesdays and leave early on Thursdays and Fridays."

"Plus with the primaries being held today I'm sure there were lots of people who went to vote before coming to work."

"Nevertheless," my father said, "there are still a large number of people who have to leave the building as quickly as possible, and without using the elevators."

"That's right, they can't use the elevators because of the fire," somebody said.

"I can't even imagine what the stairwells must look like right now," Phil said.

"Well, Phil, you're about to find out," my father said. "I'm ordering the office to evacuate the building."

"You've got to be joking," somebody else said.

"No joke," my father answered. "I'm not just in charge in this office today, I'm the fire warden for this floor. Everybody is going to leave."

"But boss, I have a report due at the end of the day," Phil said.

"It's going to be due at the end of tomorrow."

"And I have a big deal happening in just a few minutes," another man said. "It's a conference call with London and Paris."

"London and Paris are going to have to talk together without you."

"But it's my deal!" he protested.

"It's still your deal. If you leave right now you can get out of the building and re-route your line through your cellphone. Everybody, close down your computers, gather whatever you think you really need to do business from your homes–if you really, really don't think you can take a day off–and head for the stairwells."

"The stairwells?" somebody called, and others seemed to be equally confused.

"Yes, nobody is going to use the elevators."

"But it isn't *this* building that's on fire."

"Rules are rules. Elevators are not to be used in the event of an evacuation. What if they have to turn off the electricity to the complex because of the fire? Does anybody want to be trapped for the day in an elevator?" he asked.

My whole body flushed and I felt almost panicky. The idea of being trapped in an elevator was like some sort of nightmare to me. Nobody else said anything, but nobody looked happy, either.

"Come on, I'm not asking you to walk *up* eighty-five floors. Take your time. Leave, go home, spend some time with your families. Now go."

Nobody moved.

"That wasn't a suggestion," my father said. "That was an order. Everybody out, now."

People became unstuck and started hurrying off to their cubicles or offices.

"Oh!" my father yelled out. "One more thing. Call home and let people know you're okay. If they just turn on the TV they'll be worried that it's *our* tower that was hit."

I hadn't even thought about that. What would Mom think if she saw the TV? She'd be having a fit right now.

"I'll call home," I said to my father.

"Good. I'll gather up my things. You can use the phone over there," he said pointing to an empty desk. "Dial nine to get out."

I grabbed the phone and quickly punched in the numbers–I hit the wrong button. I hadn't realized until now that I was actually shaking. I hung up and started dialing again. It clicked and then started to ring.

"Come on . . . pick it up . . . be home." It kept on ringing until the answering machine kicked in.

"Mom, it's me . . . we're fine. It wasn't our building, it was the North Tower that got hit. But we're leaving anyway. We'll probably be home before you get this message. We're fine . . . bye-bye."

People were already starting to leave. They had put on their jackets, grabbed their briefcases or bags and headed toward the stairwell. I looked up at the TVs. Now every single one of them was showing scenes from the North Tower. This had to be the biggest news story of the day, and I was a witness. I shook my head. I wasn't seeing anything different from anybody else, anywhere in the world. I had to see it with my own eyes.

I slowly walked back into my father's office. He was on the phone.

"We have to redirect all our business to the L.A. office . . . Yes, I know that it won't be open for another two hours. The London office can handle things until then . . . I *know* it wasn't our tower that was hit, and no, I won't be leaving a skeleton staff. They've already left. I'll be home in about two hours. You can direct calls to me at that time . . . Yes . . . Yes, don't worry. I'll simply field calls from my house as soon as I get home. I can make up for things then and I'll work until all the important deals are dealt with . . . Yes . . . Yes, I understand that you're not happy, but it's my call. Fine . . . yes . . ."

It was obvious that while my father was going to leave he wasn't going to take the advice he'd given his staff about spending time with their families. He was just going to do his work from home. How typical. Even a plane crashing into the World Trade Center and his office being evacuated wasn't enough to stop him from working.

I eased over to the windows. I was caught by an irrational fear that somehow what was happening over at the other building would jump out across the open space and get me. That was stupid. We were here, safe, separated by the distance of the plaza.

My father finally hung up the phone. "The big boss doesn't agree with my decision. He said there was no need to take such extreme measures." He shook his head. "The old fart would have wanted us to keep working if it had been *this* tower that was hit. Let me get my things, and then we have something else to do before we leave."

Slowly I edged toward the window. I looked up. The smoke was even thicker and it didn't look as though it was just coming from four or five of the floors now. What had happened to the people on that floor when the plane hit? No, it wasn't *floor*, it was *floors*. And what was happening to those people on all the floors above the fire? Had they been able to get down the stairs, or would they be trapped up there until the firemen climbed up to save them? Could they get off from the top? Could a helicopter land up there or dangle a rope and ladder like I'd seen in movies?

"Oh my God," I gasped as I stepped back from the window. There, just before my eyes, two small figures, hand in hand, had leaped from a window.

CHAPTER SEVEN

"Will, what's wrong?" my father asked.

I backed away from the windows. I didn't want to look down. I didn't want to see what I knew had happened.

"Will, are you okay?"

I numbly nodded my head. "They . . . they . . . out of the tower . . . two people . . . they . . . they . . ." I couldn't get myself to finish the sentence. I felt like I was going to be sick. I had just seen them for a split second, and thank goodness they were too far away for me to see their faces, but I knew it was a man and a woman and they were holding hands.

My father got up from his desk and reached over and put his hands on my shoulders.

"What did you see?" he asked.

"Two people . . . they jumped from the building."

My father shook his head. "Poor souls."

"But . . . but why would they do that?"

"They must have been trapped by the fire and saw no way out. Maybe it wasn't even deliberate. Maybe they just fell. I'm just so sorry you had to see that. So sorry that you had to be here instead of safe at school."

"Safe at school . . . aren't we safe here?"

"Of course we are," he said, sounding reassuring. "I just meant safe from what you witnessed. We have to leave now."

Suzie popped her head into the doorway. "Everybody has gone."

"Even Phil?"

"Even Phil. I chased him out personally. None of the traders were too happy, though."

"Well, if they're not on the phone working a deal, they're not making money. I bet most of them will be on their cellphones talking business before they hit the base of the building," my father said. "Now I need you and Will to leave."

"What about you?" Suzie asked.

"Yeah?" I wanted an answer to that myself.

"I'm going to be a while still. I have to go to the other offices on the floor to make sure they all leave as well."

"Why do *you* have to do that?" I asked.

"I'm the fire warden for this *entire* floor. I'm responsible for the safety of everybody here."

There was that word, *safe*, again. Each time he said it I felt less safe and more concerned.

"I want to go down with you," I said.

"I'd rather you just got out of the building."

"And I'd rather stay with you. Unless you think it isn't safe in the building, and if you think that then you should come with us right now."

"It is safe. I'm just being cautious. Fine, you can stay with me and we'll hurry." He turned to Suzie. "We'll walk you to the stairwell and then you can head down and we'll quickly go to the other offices."

"You sure you don't want my help?" Suzie asked.

"The best way you can help me is to go home and start connecting to the London office. You live closer so you'll be able to make contact before I can. Let them know I'll be online by eleven."

Work, again with work. I was willing to bet he'd be on his own cellphone and taking care of business before we hit the train home.

We walked back out to the main office. It was empty and eerie. The bank of televisions had been turned off. The computer screens were blank. But the telephones never stopped ringing. We walked to the stairwell where we'd come in that morning.

"Suzie, I'll call you at eleven. Try to keep them calm," my father said.

"I thought we were all supposed to leave and take a day off?" Suzie said.

"That advice isn't for you and me. Don't you think I'd take a day off if I could?" he asked.

Before I could think to control myself I laughed out loud. The sound was so strange coming just then.

"I guess I deserve that," my father said. "I've missed a lot of days off. I've missed a lot of things. Let's do what we have to do and get out of here."

"I'll be waiting for your call," Suzie said, and she disappeared into the stairwell.

I felt a little pang of remorse. Part of me did want to just go with her and get out of the building as soon as possible. I really didn't like being there. Again, it didn't make any sense to be nervous, but I was.

Then I started to think how long it was going to take to climb down the stairs. If you could go down two floors a minute–and I didn't know if you could keep that pace up for eighty-five flights–it would take over forty minutes. Of course that would only be possible if the stairs were clear, and if every floor was evacuating then the stairwells would be incredibly crowded. People would be bumping into each other, and the slowest would be holding up everybody all the way behind them for floors and floors.

"You coming?" my father asked.

I snapped out of my trance. My father was standing at the glass doors that led out to the corridor. I could see a bank of elevators just down the way. I hurried over to him and he locked the doors behind us.

"Some people try to take advantage of situations like this to loot or rob," he said as he gave the doors a shake to make sure they were locked.

Just to the other side of the elevators was another set of almost identical glass doors. The gold letters identified it as a law firm. The lights were on, but the office looked deserted. My father gave the door a push. It was locked.

"I'm glad they made the same decision. That's good," he said.

It was looking like this was going to be easy–and fast. *That* was good. We continued down the hall. There was another door–big, solid, wooden. According to the door it was an engineering firm. I could just hope that it was locked and that they'd already–my father opened the door. I followed in after him. There were ten or eleven people huddled around a small TV. The screen was filled with the image of the tower. The smoke seemed to be thicker and blacker, staining the blue sky, almost blotting it out above the towers. It was obvious that the fire was getting stronger, and it looked as though it was spreading to other floors. Was that why those two people had jumped? Were they trapped and chose to die quickly rather than burn to death?

"Hello," my father called out and they all turned around. "Who's in charge?"

"I guess that would be me," a man said. He was wearing a suit but he was so young–maybe in his twenties–that he looked as though he had borrowed the clothes from his father.

"You?" my father asked.

The man shrugged. "All the senior partners are out today. I'm it."

"My name is John Fuller," my father began. "I work just down the hall. I've asked all my people to leave the building."

"We were talking about that," he said. "It's not like we're doing any work. It's just that I'm only a junior and I don't really have the authority to close down the office. I don't want to get in trouble."

"You won't. I'm the fire warden for this floor. I'm *ordering* you all to leave. If anybody gives you a hard time you tell them you were just following my orders."

The man shrugged again. "That works for me. Okay, everybody, gather your stuff and let's get out of here." People started to get up.

The picture on their TV screen suddenly changed from the building to a close-up of a man sitting behind a desk. "We have an update."

Everybody stopped and turned back toward the set.

"It has been confirmed that the plane that crashed into the World Trade Center was American Airlines Flight 11. It carried eighty-one passengers and a crew of eleven. It departed Boston en route to Los Angeles. It was reportedly hijacked shortly after takeoff and it can only be assumed that it was deliberately crashed into the building in an act of terrorism."

There were gasps. I felt my head spin. Somebody had deliberately crashed a plane, killing themselves and all the others on board and everybody where the plane hit . . . it was beyond belief.

"That explains the severity of the fire," one of the women said. "The fire is being fed by the jet fuel aboard the plane. A plane flying cross-country from Boston to L.A. would have had over ten thousand gallons of fuel on board. The flight to New York would have burned off less than a tenth of that. That would be some fire, an *incredibly* hot fire."

"We are now going to return live to the scene," the announcer said, "where one of our reporters is at the base of the tower, and has, standing by, an official from the Fire Department."

The screen changed again and we all stood there, transfixed, hypnotized by the TV. There was a reporter, microphone in hand, standing beside a man in a uniform. Somehow I'd expected him to be in full fire-fighting gear–and younger. He almost looked like a grandfather. Both men had serious, stern faces.

"I want to start off by saying that we have had to relocate our remote away from the plaza below the tower due to the debris that is falling. It was no longer safe to remain at that location. With me is Captain Raymond of the New York Fire Department. Captain, can you give us an update?"

"Certainly. We are in the process of evacuating the building. It is being done in a very orderly manner."

"And what can you tell us about the fire? Are your men having success in battling the blaze?"

"As yet our men have not reached the scene of the fire."

The reporter looked shocked but didn't say anything.

"Our firefighters have to climb ninety floors. We expect they will reach the site of the fire within minutes." That made me think about what my mother had said about there being no such thing as a "fat, unfit fireman." That would be a hard workout–even worse carrying a firefighter's gear. James's father was based in Manhattan–would he be one of the guys racing up ninety floors to help?

"Do you have any word of casualties?" the report asked.

"We have no official word about deaths or injuries in the building."

"Can we assume there were deaths?" the reporter asked.

"I don't want to make too many comments based on speculation at this time, but I can't imagine that there weren't some deaths on the floors where the plane hit."

"And what about the people in the floors above the fire, were they able to be evacuated?"

"Again, I have no information at this time. I just want you to know that everything that can possibly be done is being done."

"I'm sure it is," the reporter said. "Thank you for your time, Captain. And now, back to the anchor desk."

My father walked over and turned off the TV to break the trance. "It's time to stop watching and start leaving. Please, all of you, use the stairwells to evacuate."

"Stairwells?" a woman asked.

"There is no guarantee that they won't turn off the power to the buildings," my father said, "and anybody in the elevators would be stranded. Take the stairs and take your time."

"I just wish I'd worn my hiking boots instead of my high heels today," a woman said, pointing down at her very high, stiletto heels.

"Take the shoes off and go barefoot," another woman suggested.

As they all started to scramble away my father led me out of their office and back into the corridor.

"One more to go."

At the end of the hall was another office, with big glass doors.

"This one's another trading company," my father said, "like ours."

As we got closer I could see that there were still people inside. We walked in and there were dozens of them, all at their desks, working at computer terminals or talking on the phone. It was strange–nobody looked up as we entered. They all seemed to be working away, oblivious not only to us but to what was happening in the next tower.

"Excuse me!" my father called out loudly. "I need to speak to whoever is in charge."

"That would be me," a man said. He was standing beside a woman working at her desk. He was older, gray, thinning hair, dark suit, and, judging from his expression, he wasn't a happy or friendly character.

"Hello, I'm John Fuller, from down the hall," my father said. "And I'm not sure if you and your staff are aware that there has been a terrible–"

"Of course we're aware there that a plane has crashed into the North Tower," the man snapped, cutting my father off.

"Sorry, I just thought that since you were all still working that somehow you weren't."

"Can you tell me how us gawking out the window or watching TV could be of any benefit to what is happening over there?" the man demanded gruffly.

"I agree that neither would help. I'm here because your staff needs to evacuate."

"Evacuate? For what purpose? I'm sure *you* are *aware* it is the *other* building that was struck. Evacuating this building would have no benefit. In fact, it might even be harmful for those in the other tower."

"What do you mean?" my father asked. He now sounded annoyed too.

"Sending everybody out of this building, flooding into the streets and subways might slow down the evacuation from the North Tower–the place where people *really* need to leave."

I could see that everybody in the office had stopped working and they were witnessing the exchange between my father and this man.

"I can understand your position, but I disagree with it. The subways and streets can easily handle both buildings emptying–as they do each weekday at around five o'clock. You and your staff need to leave."

"The only one who's leaving is you. Get out so my staff and I can get back to work," he barked.

"I will be leaving," my father said.

I turned to him in surprise. I hadn't expected him to say that or give up so easily.

"Right after you and your staff all leave," my father continued. "I am the fire warden for this floor and I am *ordering* you to evacuate."

The man laughed. "I don't care what you are. There's only one person who gives orders in this office and you're looking at him. And now, I'm ordering *you* to get the hell out of here and leave me and my employees to get back to work."

My father had opened his mouth to speak when the lights suddenly started to flash and there was a loud *beep*, *beep*, *beep* that came from the overhead speakers.

"Your attention, please," came a man's voice. "Building Two is secure. There is no need, I repeat, no need, to evacuate Building Two."

The man in charge of the office made a scoffing sound and shot my father a look of disdain.

"If you are in the midst of evacuation, you may return to your office using the re-entry doors on the re-entry floors and the elevators to return to your floor. Again, Building Two is secure . . ."

He went on to repeat what he'd already said.

My father looked embarrassed. He wasn't used to being wrong . . . or at least to having it pointed out in such a public way. He turned and left the office and I rushed after him.

"Are we still going to leave?" I asked as I caught up.

He nodded his head. "We're going to leave. I just hope that none of my staff responds to that message. I don't care what anybody else says or thinks we should do. Our office is closed for the day."

That was more like him: stubborn and clinging to his view even when it was wrong.

"Whether the building is secure or not we all need to go. It isn't right to work while this tragedy is going on just outside our building. We will be evacuating the building."

That worked for me. I wanted to get out of there as soon as possible anyway.

Suddenly the entire building shook, and I staggered to the side, tumbling into the wall. There was the sound of smashing glass and the big front doors of my father's office shattered, exploding into a million pieces; ceiling tiles tumbled down, falling just in front of where we stood. Wide-eyed, open-mouthed, I stared at my father. His look of shock and the fear on his face sent a shiver through my body.

CHAPTER EIGHT

I pushed myself off the wall and tried to walk toward my father. My knees buckled and I put a hand against the wall to steady myself. No . . . wait . . . it wasn't my legs that were shaky . . . the whole building was swaying back and forth! The lights flickered, faded and then came back on again.

"Dad . . . what . . . what happened? What's happening?"

He looked scared. My father never looked scared. He was always calm and cool and in control. I felt even more afraid seeing *him* look afraid.

I staggered toward him as he moved toward me. He took my hand.

"What happened?" I asked again.

He shook his head. "I don't know. The building is swaying."

We stood there and I could feel the building moving, gently, back and forth. It seemed to go on forever but really it was no more than ten seconds before it came to a stop.

"Did the top of the other tower fall over . . . did it hit this building?"

"I don't know. I don't know what happened."

Still holding my hand he pulled me along the corridor toward the shattered front doors of his office. A million tiny pellets of glass crunched under our feet as we stepped through the now open doorway. There were more tiles fallen from the ceilings, wires hanging down, filing cabinets knocked over and computers smashed on the floor. My father reached up and turned on one of the TVs. The screen snapped to life. I couldn't believe what I was seeing.

"Oh, my good God," the announcer said. "I don't have the words to describe what I have just witnessed."

He didn't need words. The picture told the whole story. There wasn't just one building on fire. The second tower–the tower we were *standing in*– was on fire too! My whole body trembled, and if my father hadn't been holding my hand I think I might have crumpled to the ground.

"Just seconds ago, live, before our eyes, a second plane crashed into the South Tower of the World Trade Center," the announcer said. "Here is that dramatic footage."

The screen changed and there was a shot similar to one we'd already seen: the North Tower, on fire, smoke billowing up into the clear blue sky. Then a plane–a gigantic airplane–cut across the sky, banked slightly to one side and slammed into the South Tower, disappearing into a cloud of smoke and dust and debris! This was completely beyond my ability to comprehend.

"At 9:03, a second plane crashed into the South Tower of the World Trade Center. We saw it approach, cutting across the sky from the south, and then it just hit the building, disappearing, like it was sucked inside, converted to a gigantic ball of orange flame. There can now be no doubt: as with the first plane, this one was *deliberately* crashed into the South Tower of the World Trade Center."

My father walked right up to the TV and began running his finger down the picture of the tower. What was he doing?

He turned to me. "Floor seventy-nine or eighty."

"What about floor seventy-nine or eighty?"

"The plane hit this building at around the seventy-ninth floor . . . below us . . . we're above the crash."

I looked at him and then at the screen. Back to him again, and then my eyes settled finally on the smoke billowing out of the building. That couldn't be right. We couldn't be above because that meant we were trapped. That couldn't be.

"M-maybe you're wrong," I stammered. "It's hard to tell what floor it is because of all the smoke."

"I counted," my father said.

"Count again!"

"We do not as yet have much information about the passengers on the doomed airplane," the announcer said. "What we do know is that at 9:03 a commercial airplane crashed into the South Tower, hitting at an angle that caused damage to floors seventy-nine, eighty, eighty-one and eighty-two. Beyond that we have no information about fatalities in the buildings. And while we have no further information at this time, the pictures speak volumes. I can't imagine that anybody on those floors could have survived the impact of a fully fueled commercial airplane slamming into the side of the building.

"To recap. At 8:46, American Airlines Flight 11 out of Boston crashed into the North Tower of the World Trade Center. Any doubts that may have existed that this was an accident have been completely eliminated as, at 9:03, a second plane crashed into the South Tower in what is surely an act of terrorism . . . the worst act of terrorism in the history of this country."

My father reached up and clicked off the TV. "Now we know what happened."

My father's voice was soft, measured, reassuring. And he didn't look scared any more. He just looked as he normally did–in control, calm, cool.

"Now we have to decide what we do."

"What *can* we do?" I asked. "We're trapped. We're above the fire."

"We're above it, but that doesn't mean we're trapped."

From behind us, in the corridor, came sounds. There were people, dozens and dozens of people, the ones who had been in the office that refused to leave. I looked around for that smug, stupid man who had refused my father's order to evacuate. If he'd listened they might be safe now–safe, or dead. How far could they have gotten? Maybe they would have just made it a few floors down and they would have been somewhere on one of those floors when the plane hit. They would have been killed instantly. At least here they were still alive . . . still alive, but trapped, the way those people in the other tower were trapped . . . the way those two people were trapped who chose to jump rather than wait to be burned alive. I felt numb all over.

There were people standing in front of the elevator doors, madly pushing the button to try to call up the elevator.

"The elevators won't be coming," my father said, "and even if they did they wouldn't be safe. Everybody has to take the stairs."

Almost as one the people turned and started off down the corridor. We followed. There was a smell–a bitter, acrid smell–the smell of something burning . . . of course something was burning.

The door was pushed open. There was smoke coming out and up the stairwell! And it was already crowded with people–people climbing *up* from the lower floors. There was no noise except for the sound of feet against the stairs. Those entering from our floor started to climb up as well. I started to join in when my father grabbed me and pulled me to a halt.

"Wait," he said. He stopped somebody who was climbing. "What is it like below?"

"The way is blocked . . . smoke . . . fire . . . there's no way to get past the fire. We have to climb up, get as far away from the fire as possible and wait until the firemen come and put out the blaze."

"Thanks," my father said. "Thanks."

My father motioned for me to follow him out of the stairwell and back into the corridor. We had to move through the traffic trying to move in the other direction. Despite the urgency, the fear, the desperation, everybody was quiet and polite and orderly. There was no pushing, no bad words exchanged–hardly *any* words exchanged. I followed my father back to his office.

"What are we doing?" I demanded. "We have to get away from the fire!" I was feeling panicked. "We have to go up and get farther away from it!"

"We might decide to do that, but it might not be the best way to get away from the fire. We have to see if there are any other choices."

I was struck by the strange image of those two people jumping. That wasn't a choice.

"That man said the way down was blocked," I argued.

"It might be or it might not."

"But I could see the smoke!" I protested. "We have to climb up before the fire reaches us here."

"The smoke travels a lot faster than the fire could. These buildings are designed to contain fires so they don't spread from floor to floor."

I felt a little relief. "But shouldn't we just do what everybody else is doing and go to the top?"

"Doing what everybody else does isn't necessarily the right thing. Do you know how many times I've done the opposite of what everybody else was doing? I bought when they were selling or sold when they were buying or–"

"This isn't some stupid business deal!" I snapped. "This is our lives!"

My father placed his hands on my shoulders. "I know that. I'm not going to allow myself to panic. We have to take the time to make the right decision."

I felt like brushing his hands aside and rushing back to the stairwell and up and away from the fire. I didn't. He looked so confident, so sure of himself. He was usually right about things. He was one of the smartest people I knew.

"Okay?" he asked.

I nodded.

"Good. We're going to go back to my office. You're going to try to call your mother. We have to let her know that we're safe."

"Are we?" I asked.

He didn't answer right away and my whole spine tingled. "Let her know that we're alive . . . that we're okay for now."

I nodded again.

We went back into the office. "Use any one of those phones," my father said as he rushed off.

"Where are you going?" I asked, not wanting to let him out of my sight.

"My office. I have to get something from my desk."

My mouth dropped open. What could possibly be that important that he needed to get it right now? Even with all of this happening all around us, people dying, people *dead*, us in danger, he was still thinking about business.

I picked up the phone. There was dead air, not even a dial tone. I pushed a button, trying to find a line out. Nothing. I grabbed a second phone. It was dead as well. Feeling even more panicky I reached for a third. There was no life. I dropped it to the floor. Then I realized that my father always had his cellphone with him. We could call with that.

I walked toward his office but stopped in front of the bank of TVs. I reached up and turned one on. The screen flickered for a split second and then came to life with the scene I knew would be there. The Twin Towers stood against the skyline, thick black smoke billowing out from gaping holes. I was in the second building, the one on the left of the screen, the one with the smoke coming from lower down. I slumped down and sat on the edge of a desk, looking up at the image. It wasn't real. None of this could be real. It was like some bizarre movie, the product of some writer and Hollywood producer. I should see some interior shots of a movie star–probably playing a fireman–valiantly fighting the blaze and saving people. Or maybe a gigantic ape–King Kong–should be climbing the side of the building. Or helicopters should be plucking people from the roof . . . could they do that?

"We can now confirm that there have been dozens and dozens of deaths," the unseen announcer said. "There have been numerous people, including members of the Fire Department and people fleeing the buildings, who have been killed by falling debris from the towers. A hailstorm of concrete and steel continues to rain down upon the plaza and surrounding streets."

The camera changed to a shot of the plaza. It was littered with hunks of metal and stone. There was a police car, almost unrecognizable, crushed by a gigantic hunk of concrete.

"All emergency personnel in the city have been recalled, as have doctors and nurses and all health professionals. Hospitals are preparing for the mass of casualties that is expected. Fire officials have indicated that they now have their first firefighters at the scene of the blaze in the North Tower. They are confident that they can safely evacuate all people below the level of the fire."

But what about those *above* the fire? And what about the people in *this* building? People like us? Had anybody reached the fire in our building yet? No, of course they hadn't, because it had just happened.

"Did you get your mother?" my father asked.

"The lines are dead. Can you call her on your cell?"

He shook his head. "I can't get service. Everybody's trying to call and the cell towers are overwhelmed. We'll keep trying. What are they saying?" he asked, gesturing to the TV.

"They're just showing the towers and the people getting out."

"I hope my staff got out."

I looked at my watch. It was eight minutes after nine. Twenty or twenty-five minutes had passed. "Not yet," I said. "If they were going at the same speed as us when we came down from the Observation Deck they'd still be on the stairs."

"You're right, and they couldn't possibly be moving as fast as we moved. The stairwells probably became pretty crowded–"

"And now we have, by phone," the television announcer said, "one of the consulting engineers for the construction of the World Trade Center."

My father reached up and increased the volume.

"Shouldn't we be going to . . . wherever we're going?" I asked.

"We need to have as much information as possible to make the right decision. Just a few seconds."

I felt my heart pounding in my chest. I felt like I had to go somewhere, anywhere, and not just stand there doing nothing . . . but what choice did I have?

"Are you there, Mr. McGregor?" the announcer asked.

"Yes, I am," a voice replied. It was obvious that it was coming over a phone line.

"Can you comment on the scene you are seeing on the screen?" the announcer said.

"It's hard to believe. The amount of smoke is simply unbelievable."

"I was informed that the buildings were designed in such a way as to contain and control fire on any floor," the announcer said.

"They were, and that is a life-saving measure in this case. The smoke you see . . . the fuel feeding these flames is not from the building itself but from the jet fuel that was on the planes."

"It would certainly be hard to design a building for such an occurrence–a direct hit from an airplane."

"Actually," the engineer said, "the buildings *were* designed to withstand an airplane crash. We did tests, simulations of a private plane crash."

"A private plane? Like a Cessna?" the announcer asked.

"Larger. Two-engine prop plane."

"But nothing like this. You didn't test for the impact of a large commercial airliner?"

"No," the engineer said. "We didn't test for something that we couldn't conceive happening. This is beyond anything we ever imagined."

Once again my father reached up and clicked off the set. "He's not saying anything that can help us make our decision. It's time to leave. We'll continue to try to get your mother by cellphone."

"Did you get what you needed from your office?" I asked.

"I did." He pulled a tie out of his pocket. I recognized it. I had given it to him for his birthday a month ago.

"You went there to get that tie?"

"It's one of the things I got. It's my favorite tie. And that's going to make this hurt even more."

He took the tie and ripped the back, opening it up.

"What . . . what are you doing?"

"Making a mask for you. Here, let me get it wet." He bent over and put it under the spout of the water cooler, drenching it with water. He handed it to me. "If it gets smoky you can tie this over your mouth and nose."

The smoke . . . the fire. Somehow now the fact that he'd destroyed my gift didn't seem so bad.

He took the tie from around his neck and did the same with it.

"I also want you to take this," he said, holding something out for me.

"A whistle?" I said, taking it from him.

"It's part of my fire warden equipment. That and this flashlight." He pulled a small yellow flashlight out of his pocket. "I want you to slip the whistle around your neck."

"Why would I want a whistle?" I asked.

"In case we get separated you can blow the whistle and I can find you."

"But why would we get separated?" I felt panicky.

"We won't, but I just don't know. It could be dark, things could happen . . . and if they do–and they won't–you blow the whistle and I'll find you

. . . you know I'll do whatever I need to do to find you."

I looked at the whistle. If I'd had this whistle years before could I have made him show up at my games? Would he have been home more often, been there to help me with my homework? Nope, it was just a little orange plastic whistle. To do that it would have had to be magical.

"Now take a big drink of water."

"I'm not thirsty."

"This might be your last chance to get water for hours. Just take a drink."

He had a point. I grabbed a cup, filled it and slugged down the water.

"Okay, let's go. We're going to try to find a way down."

CHAPTER NINE

"Should we be going that way?" I asked my father, pointing down the corridor to the door to the stairs where everybody had been going down.

"No," he said, shaking his hand. "If we believe what they said on the TV–that the plane hit the south side of the building–then we need to try the stairwell farthest away from the point of impact."

I trailed my father back to the stairs that we had originally come down in the morning. My father put his hands against the door to the stairwell. He just stood there. Was it locked or was he having second thoughts about doing this or–?

"The door is cool," my father said. "That means there's no fire directly behind it. Here we go."

I took a deep breath and held it. I braced myself, anticipating what might be in the stairwell. He opened the door up so I could see clearly. There was nothing. No people, no fire. But there was smoke–not thick but drifting upward.

"Come on," my father said.

I hesitated. For a split second I thought about refusing to go into the stairwell with him, but I couldn't do that. If I had to trust somebody, it was going to be him.

The stairwell was gray, concrete and somehow darker than when we'd come down that morning. The smoke wasn't bad, not overwhelming. What was worse was the smell. It was a bitter, acrid odor that permeated the air and filled my nostrils.

"It's a good sign that nobody's here," my father said.

"It is?" I thought a good sign would be people going *down* the stairs.

"I was hoping we wouldn't see people climbing up or stalled here in the stairwell."

"But why is there nobody here?"

He shook his head. "Maybe people have already gone up or down through this stairwell."

"So you think we can get down, that we can get through those floors?" I asked.

"I wish I could just say yes, but I don't know. I'm hoping . . . I'm hoping. If we can get down anywhere it'll be through this stairwell. It would be protected by the elevator shafts and the other two stairwells. This is our best chance."

"This is our only chance," I blurted out, saying what I was thinking and almost hearing the words before I'd thought them.

"No, not necessarily our only chance."

"What other chance is there?" I asked.

"There might be other options, things I haven't thought of yet. But for now let's just check out *this* option."

It wasn't just my imagination, it was darker than I remembered it on our trip down that morning. Some of the lights were off. Others were shattered by the impact, and little grains of glass littered the floor.

"Keep a hand on the railing and stay a few steps behind me. Not too many, but not too close."

"Why?" I asked.

"Just do what I say," he ordered.

My father turned on the flashlight. I noticed that there were glowing white strips on the handrails and the edges of the steps that brightly reflected the light. I took a few steps and then hesitated. I thought about what we were walking toward. Now, suddenly, all of this had the potential to be terribly real. This was no longer just in the other building–or really more like a *picture* of the other building on TV–this was here, and now and right under my feet. An airplane–a fully loaded, fully fueled jet commercial plane–had crashed into this building no more than thirty or forty feet beneath my feet . . . so close, and it would get closer with each step that I took. We weren't talking about injuries or fatalities like they were just a bunch of numbers. There were real people, real flesh-and-blood people who had been on that plane and in those offices just below us who were now dead . . . dead or horribly injured . . . burned . . . mangled.

I just stood there, one foot on the first step, one foot on the landing, holding on to the railing, frozen in place.

"Okay, that's far enough behind," my father said, "you can come now."

A shiver went through my entire body, unlocking my legs, and I started down the steps after him. He was five or six steps ahead of me and had just reached the first landing. He looked back at me as he made the turn and went around the corner. I felt a rush of panic that he was leaving me behind and I jumped down two steps and then a second pair and a third, hitting the landing with a solid thud, spinning around the corner to continue down.

I reached up to my forehead. I'd wrapped the tie around my forehead like a bandana. It was wet and cold. It was also my mask if I needed it. I could slip it over my nose and mouth and breathe through the material, and it would filter out smoke and fumes. I felt a little reassured, and then even more unsettled when I realized that I was relying on a ripped, wet, not even very expensive tie to protect me from a raging fire caused by the crash of an airplane carrying tons of burning jet fuel. This was ridiculous. We should have just headed back up and waited for the firemen to put out the blaze.

"Let's have a peek," my father said as he went to pull open the door on the floor below us, checking first to make sure it wasn't hot. There was a big "84" on the back.

He pulled it open. "Hello!" he yelled, and I practically jumped backwards up the steps.

Instead I bounded down until I was standing beside him, peering through the door. I felt like a peeping tom, looking into a place where I didn't belong. The office was not much different from the one we'd left a flight above. There were overturned desks and chairs, shattered glass and paper everywhere, some ceiling tiles on the floor and others hanging from the ceiling, cabinets knocked over and, strangest of all, a cup of coffee, still steaming, sitting on the closest desk. Imagine that, just a few minutes ago somebody was sitting at that desk, maybe worried about what was happening in the next building but still enjoying their morning coffee, and then . . .

"Hello!" my father called out again. "Is anybody here?"

Complete silence. Not even ringing phones. The phones on that floor must have been out of order too. Probably all the phones above the fire were gone.

"Hopefully they evacuated before the crash," my father said.

"I hope."

"Let's get going." He let the door swing closed and he started down to the next level. I looked at my watch. It was 9:17. My father got partway down the flight and I started after him. Hitting the landing I made the turn and realized it was now much darker. The lights on the landing and on the next level down were mainly broken, and the one remaining fluorescent tube was flickering and hardly throwing out any light at all. In the top corner of the walls there were small lamps–battery-operated emergency lights–trying to light the way. They were much dimmer than the regular lights.

My father aimed his flashlight down the stairs. The bulb that had seemed so weak in the office now projected a strong, powerful shaft of light.

"Watch out for the glass from the smashed lights," my father said.

Reaching the landing I heard–and felt–the broken glass crunching under my shoes.

"Eighty-three," my father said. "We're getting closer."

"Do you think the smoke is getting thicker?" I asked anxiously.

"Maybe a little, but not that much," he said. "But look at the light."

The flashlight was pointed down the stairs. Drifting through the beam was a thick layer of smoke. It slowly danced, climbing through the shaft of light and then vanishing into the darkness. I reached up and touched the tie around my forehead. It was my security blanket.

It was even darker below where we stood. Not even the emergency lights were working.

"Stay closer to me," my father said.

We started down to the next level. I stayed right on his heels, only one step back, looking around him, following the beam of light as much as I was following him. It felt better anyway to be close to him. I held on to the railing, although I would have liked to hold my father's hand instead. I started to count the stairs. Nine steps, then a landing, a turn and down nine more stairs.

We made the next landing–"82" was marked on the back of the door. I wondered if my father was going to open the door and poke his head in. We really didn't have time to stop at every floor. I was glad when he just made the turn and started down to the next level. It was just as dark down there. What would we have done if my father hadn't had that flashlight, and what would we do if something happened to it? I didn't need to think of that. There was enough right in front of me to worry about without making up anything new.

Within a few steps it became obvious that the smell and the smoke were getting stronger and thicker. My father let the beam drift up to the ceiling of the stairwell. There, at the very top, was a thick stream of smoke.

"As long as it stays up there we're fine," my father said.

I looked down to the next landing–floor eighty-one–we were now one or two floors above where the plane had hit. Maybe it was dark, and there was more smoke, but it was still okay if we just–

"The floor is all wet," my father said.

I stepped down onto the sopping-wet floor. "What is it? Where is it coming from?"

My father pushed open the door. There was a loud hissing sound. The sprinklers had all been activated and water was raining down from the ceiling! The scene below was a sopping, soaking mass of overturned filing cabinets, computers smashed on the floor–the floor . . . it was uneven . . . it was rippled, buckled. The floor looked as if it had been crunched, pushed up. There were ceiling tiles down and speakers, attached by wires, swaying gently back and forth. All the overhead lights were off–either smashed or turned off–but the scene was still visible by natural light. The few windows I could see in the distance were smashed. Along with the hissing of the sprinklers was the faint whistling of wind coming in through the broken glass.

My father let the door close and we started down again.

The water from the sprinklers was flowing down the stairs, making them slippery. Maybe it made our footing a little bit less sure, but if fire was our problem then surely water was something that could only help.

I bumped into my father and startled. Why had he stopped? I looked beyond him and saw the reason. The way was blocked. It looked as though the walls of the stairwell had collapsed, caved in. End of the line. It was time to go back up.

"Hold this," my father said, handing me the flashlight. "Keep the beam right where it is."

I watched as he placed his hands against the obstruction. He pushed and it seemed to give slightly.

"It's drywall," he said. "It's collapsed off the walls."

He drew back his foot and gave it a kick. The panel buckled and then, as he kicked it again, snapped in two! He knocked it out of the way. Another piece was right against it. He kicked and punched and then muscled it to the side. As it gave way a cloud of smoke billowed out from behind it. The smoke that had been trapped behind the obstruction was now flowing freely up the stairwell! My heart jumped into my throat!

"Make sure the tie covers your mouth!" my father yelled.

I fumbled with the bandana and pulled it into place. My father did the same with his. It felt cold and I was having trouble drawing in air through the material, but somehow, it was working. The air seemed cleaner and the horrible smell was less, but nothing was protecting my eyes–they burned and stung, and even the tears that came didn't bring relief.

"Stay low," my father said.

I dropped down to one knee and my pants became instantly soaked. "We have to go back," I pleaded.

"Not yet," my father said. "It's still okay." My father took the flashlight from me and aimed the light down to the landing below. There was some debris–pieces of the drywall my father had smashed–on the stairs, but the way was basically clear. We stepped around them and down to the eightieth-floor landing.

"Ouch!" my father yelled as he jumped backwards, almost bumping into me.

"What happened? What's wrong?" I exclaimed.

"My hand," he said, holding it up. "I burned it when I touched the door. It's red hot! The whole floor is on fire. Look." He pointed the flashlight down to the bottom of the door. There was smoke streaming out from underneath and there was a strange reddish light . . .

I suddenly realized that I was feeling really hot, it was extremely hot here . . . but why shouldn't it be?

"Should we head back up now?"

"If we need to get back up we can . . . we might have to . . . but not now . . . not yet."

We started down again. There were pieces of glass mixed in with parts of the broken drywall. The stairs were soaked and slick. There was a little river of water now flowing down the steps.

"It stinks here," I said.

My father bent down and touched his finger against the liquid and then brought it up to his face. "This isn't just water. It's got the jet fuel mixed in."

"We're standing in gasoline?" I asked in shock.

"Mixed with water. Water doesn't burn," he said, answering my unasked fear.

He started moving again before I could even think to object. It wouldn't have made any difference anyway. Whether I wanted to give up didn't matter. My father was determined to keep going until he couldn't go any farther.

The smoke seemed to be getting stronger with each step that we took. The whole top of the stairwell was now filled with a virtual river of smoke, flowing, bumping, bubbling along. Thank goodness there was still a foot or two of clear, open air between my head and the smoke. I bent down slightly anyway and adjusted the bandana, which was slipping down off my nose.

"Not much farther," my father said. He started to cough violently. The fumes–the stench–were becoming even more overwhelming. "A floor or two, or maybe three, and we're through it."

He stopped at the landing and trained the light down at the seventy-ninth floor. It was already bright down there. The door was bent and buckled and the doorframe itself was knocked away from the wall. There was angry red light shining and flickering through the gaps, smoke pouring out and up. And there was a sound . . . the sound of a fire burning, raging.

"Stay as far away from the door as you can, and stay low," my father said very quietly in my ear.

Why was he whispering? Did he think the fire would hear us and react? That made no sense, but still . . . somehow it didn't seem like a bad idea. He started down and I stayed right on his heels, hugging the wall, holding the handrail, bending over so I was above the soaked and running floor but below the steaming, smoking ceiling.

The heat coming from behind the door was phenomenally hot. I could feel it scorching the side of my face. I put a hand up to block the heat and I turned my head away, quickly rounding the corner. Instantly the heat faded, shielded by the concrete wall, although the eerie red light still illuminated the whole area.

"Is that it?" I gasped. "Are we past it?"

My father shook his head. He pointed the flashlight up. There was more smoke coming up the stairs. There was still more fire below us.

I felt a wave of disappointment wash over me, and my knees felt tired and weak. I just wanted to sit down . . . sit down, curl up and cry. But this was the worst place in the world to stop. Here we were, on the stairwell, *between* the floors that were on fire. Disappointment was pushed aside by fear, and that fear gave me a surge of energy. It wasn't ending here, I wouldn't let it.

My father stopped again on the landing between the two floors. The whole floor was flooded with water. Somehow the floor had buckled up and the water–the *liquid*–was pooling before cascading down below. There had to be three or four inches of water on the floor. My father trained the flashlight on the door–we were at the seventy-eighth floor. The door was bent, buckled at the bottom, but intact–more than on the floor above. There was smoke streaming out of the gaps at the top and the sides of the door and water pouring out from the bottom. There were more pieces of drywall knocked off the wall, partially blocking our way, and the whole wall–the concrete wall–was cracking and fractured. Chunks of it were littering the stairs. A pipe jutted out of the wall and water poured out of it. We stood there on the landing, suspended between the two floors, fire above us, fire below us. We couldn't just stand there forever.

"Turn sideways, facing away from the fire and toward the wall," my father said.

I followed his direction and example. Slowly we picked our way down the stairs. One step at a time . . . nine steps to a landing . . . two landings to a floor . . . seventy-eight floors to go. Heat was radiating up at us. With each step it seemed to get stronger. I tried to press my face right up to the concrete and brought my hand up to offer some protection. The air was thick with fumes and smoke and heat and sounds–the sound of water running down the stairs under my feet and the crackling, roaring noise of the fires raging above and below us. The heat, the sounds, the smells . . . this was what Hell had to be like.

I could feel the heat against the side of my face and right through the back of my head, right through the clothes on my back. I kept sliding down the wall, step by step. I turned my face even farther away from the heat of the fire so I was actually looking back at where we'd come, back up the stairs. There couldn't be that many more steps. I hit the landing and quickly spun around, made the turn and stumbled down the first few steps.

My father was just a few steps farther down. He reached up and wrapped an arm around my shoulders.

"You okay?" he asked.

I nodded. "I'm fine . . . you?"

"I feel like I've been baked and broiled, but I'm still not cooked. I think we're past the worst of it now."

"Really?"

"Really." He aimed the beam down the stairs. "It looks almost clear . . . not much smoke at all."

I looked at the light. It *was* almost clear, just some traces of smoke, a faint trail, a few wisps at the very top by the roof of the stairwell. I wanted to believe what he was saying was true, but I couldn't let myself believe it yet.

My father's hand slipped off my shoulder and he grabbed my hand. We started down the stairs. Almost instantly it became cooler. Hitting the next landing and making the turn it quickly got darker as well. The flashlight beam was our only light. There was no light from the fire. The darkness, which had scared me five floors up, was now welcoming and reassuring. I'd be happy to be guided by only the flashlight until we hit the lobby. The glow strips on the handrail and the edges of the steps flashed brightly.

"Seventy-seven," my father said and made the turn down.

The door looked to be solidly in the frame, no buckling, no bending, no fractures. There was no light coming from underneath, no smoke seeping out. Tentatively I reached out my hand and touched the door. It was cold–stone cold. There was no fire behind that door . . . we were past the fire! The air was clean and clear. There was still the smell of smoke, the bitter odor, but it was nothing like what we'd faced one floor up.

I felt a wave of relief wash over my entire body. I wanted to laugh out loud, but I didn't. I knew that we'd made it, but what about the other people, the people who had been on those floors when the plane hit . . . what had happened to them? Of course I knew. Anybody who had been there was gone, dead, incinerated or smashed into a million pieces. Nobody could have survived the impact. Nobody.

I didn't want to think about that yet.

I followed my father as he rounded the corner and we continued down the stairs. He was right to keep moving. We were past the fire floors but we were still a long way from being out of the building.

We hit seventy-six. No heat, no smoke, but the fumes were still strong. In the corner of the landing the emergency light was shining. We turned the corner and headed down again. Floor seventy-five was just below. There, on the landing, a single fluorescent bulb glowed out a welcome. I couldn't help but smile. Again, there was no hint of fire. Down below at the next landing the lights were all on and working.

"I guess I don't need this now," my father said, and he turned off the flashlight. "Or this." He pulled the bandana down around his neck. I followed suit and took a deep breath. The air felt good going into my lungs.

"The stairwell . . . it's empty . . . nobody . . . not even the sounds of anybody from below," I said. "Why?"

"I think that anybody who was on the floors below the impact zone got out right away, and anybody who was on those floors . . . well . . ."

He didn't need to finish that thought.

Strange, we were just a few floors below where it all happened, and if it hadn't been for the water still flowing down the stairs along with us there wouldn't have been anything out of the ordinary. Other than the smell and the water there was nothing that even hinted at what was happening just above our heads and all around us. It seemed just like the trip we'd made down from the Observation Deck that morning.

I looked at my watch. It was eighteen minutes after nine. Less than ninety minutes after we had been up there on the Observation Deck, staring down at the city on a beautiful, sunny September morning. Not a cloud in the sky. Less than thirty-five minutes since that first plane hit and that brilliant blue sky was stained by billowing black smoke. Less than twenty minutes since the second plane rocked this building, changing everything. We were no longer just watching the drama unfolding through the window and on the television screens; it had pushed right into our world, almost killing us. And now, here in the stairwell, we'd dodged that bullet, passed through the fire, and we were free, we were fine, we were alive!

My father stopped as we came to the next floor. There was a big number seventy-four on the back of the door.

"I was thinking," my father said, "about those people who climbed up instead of going down."

In the rush of emotions and fears, and then the relief I'd felt when we'd gotten through it, I hadn't thought about them at all. How many people had decided to move up the stairs instead of down? It had to be dozens and dozens . . . maybe hundreds.

"If they knew that this way was passable they could get down," my father said. "If only they knew. If only somebody could tell them."

"But anybody who knows has already gone down, like us, and there's no way they'd go back up and . . ." I stopped myself. He couldn't be considering what I was thinking he was thinking.

"I thought that maybe I should go back up," my father said.

I gasped. "You can't be serious!"

He shook his head. "I thought about it, but, no. Those floors that we passed were burning badly, and the fires were getting stronger, fast, judging by the way the smoke was getting thicker. Just because we got through then doesn't mean people could get through again in thirty or forty minutes."

"Forty minutes!"

"It would take me at least that long to climb up thirty floors, find them and convince a crowd of strangers–a crowd of frightened strangers–to follow me down and through the fire."

"If you could convince them at all," I said.

"You're right. Maybe I couldn't. Besides, they might not even be there now."

"What do you mean?" I asked. In my mind I saw again those two people plummeting by the window.

"There is a third stairwell. We don't know if it's passable," my father said, "but maybe it's even better and everybody has evacuated down that one."

"I hadn't thought of that." I felt relieved.

"Or perhaps they're now taking people off the roof by helicopter," he said.

"Do you think that could happen?"

"It's more of a possibility on this building because it doesn't have the communications tower at the top. There's even a helicopter pad."

"There is?" Why hadn't he told me that before? We could have gone up and waited for evacuation.

"But it hasn't been used for years. I'm not even sure it's still functional. Besides, with all the smoke I doubt a helicopter could land, and if it could the last thing they'd need is one more person to evacuate."

"Don't you mean two more?" I said, pointing at myself.

"One. If I *was* going back up it would have been by myself. I'm not risking your life."

"And I wouldn't have let you go up without me."

"I thought of that. Besides, I didn't think I could let you go anywhere without me. You're more important than anything in this building . . . anything in this world."

I felt taken aback by what he'd said. I guess I sort of knew he thought that, but to hear him say it out loud was different.

"So, it's decided. We have to keep going down. Together. I just hope we can let somebody know–the police or the Fire Department–so they can get up the stairs or get a message up to the people up top, just in case this was the only way down."

I felt a renewed sense of relief. There was no way I wanted my father to go back up there by himself, and there was no way that I was going back up there with him. I knew my father well enough to know that he wasn't just saying empty words. He had really been contemplating, figuring, planning what needed to be done to help those people, including that stupid guy who hadn't listened to him, who had basically taunted him and refused to evacuate. He didn't deserve to be saved . . . but he didn't deserve to die, either.

"We'll just go down as fast as possible. We'll keep on trying to get a call out, or maybe we'll meet some emergency personnel coming up the tower and we can tell them."

I thought back to the interview with the fire captain. It was going to be a long time before any firefighters would be able to climb this high.

"We'll just go down a few more floors and then try to find a phone that–"

My father stopped mid-sentence. He'd heard what I'd heard–or thought I'd heard: a faint voice calling out.

CHAPTER

TEN

We both stood there, no words exchanged, knowing that we had to silently wait and listen. It came again, a voice. Soft and barely audible but there.

"I think it's coming from the offices on this floor," my father said, pointing at the door.

He reached over and put a hand against the door. We both knew that the door would be cool, but I was glad he was being careful. He grabbed the handle and went to open the door but it wouldn't budge. He pulled harder.

"Is it locked?"

"It could be, but I don't think so. I think it's jammed," he said.

The door itself looked fine, no buckles or bends or dents, but the frame seemed crooked, as though the wall had shifted over.

"Help me. Grab the handle."

I grabbed on to it beneath his hands.

"Now, on three. One, two, *three*!"

I strained with all my might and the door held firm. I put my foot against the wall and used my entire body to try to muscle it and–it popped open, sending me flying backwards, my grip on the handle the only thing that saved me from tumbling down the stairs. I put a hand down on the soaking-wet landing and got to my feet.

I peered through the doorway. It was darker than in the stairwell and it was difficult to see clearly what was there. Suddenly a beam of light stretched out and through the darkness. My father had turned on his flashlight.

"Unbelievable," I mumbled as my father let the light play around the room.

There was a scene of complete devastation. It looked as if a tornado had rushed through the place. The floor was littered with what had once been the ceiling. Tiles and wires and large pieces of metal ductwork–the heating and air conditioning vents–were lying on the floor. Up above were ugly, open, raw concrete and a mass of wires. There was water seeping through the ceiling and falling to the floor like a series of small waterfalls. And there was a breeze against my face–not strong, but a stream of fresh, clean air. Obviously at least some of the windows had been smashed. Probably *all* of the windows had been smashed.

My father shone the light in front of him.

"There's smoke!" I yelled in alarm. I could see it drifting through the air in the beam of light.

"No, not smoke . . . dust," he said.

Dust? Why would there be dust? I took a deep breath. He was right, it didn't smell of smoke.

"It's from the ceiling panels or the concrete or something . . . I don't know."

There was dust drifting, suspended in the air. It was unreal, sort of like a haze or mist or fog . . . inside a building.

My father walked through the doorway and I hesitated for an instant but followed after. I stopped just inside, holding the door open with one hand and reaching for an overturned chair. I grabbed the chair and put it in the doorway to stop the door from closing. I didn't want anything to prevent us from getting back out.

"Hello!" my father called out. "Is there anybody–?"

"Here . . . here," a faint voice replied.

"Where? Where are you?" my father answered as he waved the beam around the room.

"Here . . . here." The voice was female and foreign and frightened.

"Where? I can't see you!"

"Here . . . I here!"

My father aimed the flashlight in the direction he thought the voice was coming from. There was nobody, nothing–no, there was a hand waving from beneath some debris. We rushed over. It was a little girl! What would a little girl be doing here by herself? No, it wasn't a girl, it was a small Chinese woman, lying on the floor beside a desk. She shielded her eyes from the glare of the light. Her clothes were soaking wet and there was a large gash on the side of her head.

"Are you all right?" my father exclaimed.

"Hurt . . . hurt," she whimpered. "Trapped . . . hurt."

In the edges of the beam I saw that she was pinned beneath a fallen file cabinet. There was a large piece of metal ductwork that had smashed into the desk and ceiling tiles were scattered all around her. Had one of those hit her and caused that gash?

"Hold this," my father said, passing me the flashlight.

I took the light and tried to keep it on target, away from her face and down at where she was pinned beneath the filing cabinet. My father struggled to move it, lifting it slightly away from her body.

"Pull her out," he said. I could hear the strain in his voice.

I put the flashlight onto the edge of a desk and the beam of light shifted, leaving him and her in only partial light. I reached over and pulled, helping her shift away, scuttle a few inches until her leg came free. I held on, helping her to her feet and settling her into a chair.

"Are you okay?" my father asked.

"No speak . . . much . . . English."

"Your head, does it hurt?" my father asked.

She looked confused, as though she had no idea what he was talking about–which I guess she didn't. My father put his finger to his head in the spot on her head where it was gashed.

She reached up and touched the wound, then wrenched in pain. She brought her hand back down and looked at the blood. She looked shocked, as though somehow she hadn't been aware that she was hurt there.

"What . . . what happened?" the woman asked. It was clear that she was struggling to find the words.

"I think something fell from the ceiling and hit you," he said. "Maybe something like that," he said, pointing at the piece of ductwork that lay on the desk. It was huge and heavy and angular. If that had hit her directly it would have taken her head right off her shoulders.

"But why . . . why fell?"

"An airplane hit the building." He held his arms out like the wings of a plane.

"This place?" she asked, sounding confused and shocked.

"Yes, this building. We have to get moving. Can you walk?"

She just shook her head, again, not understanding his question. He mimicked walking, moving his feet up and down in place, but she just looked even more confused.

He reached over and pulled her to her feet.

"No! No! Hurt!" she yelled. She pointed down to her leg.

I trained the beam on her lower body. Her leg was ripped open and raw and swollen! My father eased her back into the chair and then bent down to look at the leg.

"It could be broken," he said, "but even if it isn't she can't walk on it, she probably can't even put any weight on it."

"But if she can't walk, do we leave her here?" I asked.

"We can't leave her here. I don't know how safe it is."

I looked up at the open ceiling. I didn't like the water seeping through. If water could get through, if the floor had been fractured or weakened, then maybe more chunks or pieces could still fall down. I anxiously scanned the ceiling right above our heads. There was nothing there that could fall down–just open pieces of concrete. We were okay . . . okay unless the *whole* thing fell down on our heads. Was that a possibility? I didn't know, but I knew I didn't want to stay there any longer to find out.

"We have to get out of here," I said. "Soon, fast."

"You're right. We can't stay."

My father bent down in front of the woman so his face was right at the same level as hers. How was he going to explain to her that we were leaving? We could send help back but that would take time, a long time, and if I didn't feel that it was safe for us to be here for even another minute, why did I think it was okay to leave her here?

"I'm going to pick you up," my father said to her.

"You're going to carry her?" I asked.

"I don't see any other choice," he said to me. He turned back to her. "It might hurt, but we have to move. I hope you understand." His voice was calm and reassuring.

He stood up and then reached over and picked her up from the chair and cradled her in his arms. She cried out in pain but didn't fight or argue. I think she understood.

My father was a big man and she was tiny. She couldn't have weighed any more than a hundred pounds, soaking wet, and she *was* soaking wet.

"Lead the way back to the stairwell," he said. "Make sure I can see the way under my feet. I don't want to trip or drop her."

I shone the light forward, marking the entire route toward the stairs, and then mentally marked it. I got up, led the way and then trained the light backwards, behind me, to illuminate the path for my father.

"Be careful here," I said. I picked up a chair and tossed it out of his path, shoved a desk over with my hip and cleared the way as best I could.

I kicked away the chair I'd used to prop open the door to the stairwell. It was much brighter there. My father took the woman and set her down gently on the stairs. He pulled the bandana–the shredded tie–from around his neck and carefully placed it against the gash on her head. In the brighter light I could see that the cut was deep and angry and her hair was soaked and smeared with blood. Thank goodness the blood had almost stopped flowing.

Her eyes looked glazed over. She looked stunned, like she was in shock. Was that because of the head injury, or was it just because she couldn't get her mind around what was taking place? Without language I couldn't find out which it was. Either way, what did we do with her now?

"It's safer here," I said. We could just leave her now that we'd gotten her out from beneath the cabinet and onto the stairs. "Maybe the people who were on her floor have already told the authorities and somebody's on the way to get her," I said.

"I don't think so," my father answered. "My guess is that in the confusion, in the darkness, in the panic to escape nobody even noticed that she was still there. I can't imagine anybody knowing and deciding to leave her behind. That would be inhumane to leave somebody like that!"

After what I'd been thinking I suddenly felt bad.

"In all the confusion–the ceiling falling down, the lights going out, the windows smashing–I just think people rushed out and there was no way for anybody to know, or not know, who had gotten out and who remained. It would have just been pandemonium."

"I guess so. At least she's better off here than she was there."

"But not as good as she's going to be," my father said. He stood up. "I want you to help her climb onto my back."

"You're going to piggyback her down the stairs?" I asked, not believing what he was suggesting.

"I think that would be the easiest way to carry her."

"But down seventy-four flights of stairs? That's . . . that's . . . impossible!"

"I don't know how many flights I'm going to carry her, but every floor down and away from the fire is a good one. You're supposed to evacuate at least three or four floors away from a fire in both directions. We'll just take it bit by bit, stair by stair, floor by floor."

I helped the woman to her feet–actually, her foot. She kept the other foot off the ground. My father turned around and then took her arms and wrapped them around his neck. He reached back and grabbed her, lifting her up and on to his back.

"She hardly weighs anything," he said. "You lead."

"Sure." I was just happy to be moving again.

"And if I stumble, you have to try to stop me–us–from falling down."

"Yeah, sure, I can do that," I said.

I started down, looking back over my shoulder at my father. Her arms were wrapped around his neck and her little head peeked out from beside his head, but the rest of her was completely blocked by my father's body. He was a tall man, and big. Funny, as I'd grown it seemed that he wasn't nearly as big as I once thought he was. When I was little he was like a giant. I remembered when he used to carry me around on his back like he was carrying this woman . . . this woman . . . what was her name?

I turned around. "I'm Will," I said in a loud voice, pointing at myself. "And that is my father, John."

She nodded. "John and Vill," she said.

Vill was close enough.

"Ting."

"Your name is Ting?" I asked, and she nodded.

"Hello, Ting," my father said. "It's good for me to know the name of the person I'm carrying."

The stairs were clean and bright and the air was clear and fresh. Not only wasn't there any smoke, there wasn't even any hint–no smell, no fumes, nothing. There was still some water coming down the stairs but it was just a stream, not the flood that had been pouring down higher up.

We rounded another landing, then another and another. My father seemed to be moving effortlessly. Ting was tiny, and we were heading down, but still, how long could he keep this up? He had to be starting to get tired, and if he got tired that would mean that he'd be more likely to stumble or fall. I looked back with renewed awareness. I didn't know if I could catch them–there had to be close to three hundred and fifty pounds between them–but I was going to try my best.

I hit another landing, floor sixty-seven. In just a few minutes we had come down eight flights.

"You okay?" I asked my father as he reached the landing.

"I'm good for a little while longer."

His face was red and peppered with sweat. As I watched, Ting reached down with her sleeve and wiped his forehead.

"Thank you," my father said.

"Welcome."

"How are you doing up there?" my father asked. "Are you okay?"

"Okay."

"Good, then let's keep going," he said.

"You sure you don't want to stop for a while?" I asked.

"Stopping means having to start again. As long as I keep going, I figure gravity will keep me moving in the right direction."

"You know, I could carry her for a while," I suggested.

"You?"

"Why not me? I'm almost as big as you and my knees are a whole lot better," I snapped.

"You won't get any argument from me on that. Let me go a few more floors, take a break, and then we'll talk about it."

I reached the next landing and went to turn the corner. But there was no corner to turn . . . the stairs just ended! There was a door leading off to the sixty-sixth floor but only a solid concrete wall where the stairs down should have been!

CHAPTER ELEVEN

I didn't wait to say anything to my father. There was a door and no stairs, and what if that door was locked or jammed or blocked somehow? Slowly I walked over and put my hand against it. Cool . . . cold. Whatever was behind the door wasn't on fire. I knew that, but I had to check. I pushed against the bar. The door opened effortlessly. Stretching before me was a hallway. It had a concrete floor and was well lit. At the end was a gray metal door, just like the one I'd just opened. Was *it* locked?

"Stay right here!" I ordered my father. "And hold the door open!"

I raced down the hall. Sometimes doors opened from one direction but not the other. I didn't want to somehow get trapped between the two. I jumped into the next door and practically merged into it as my weight and force propelled me into the unmoving metal. It didn't budge, it was locked! This was it. We were trapped and . . . I looked down. It was a *pull* door, not a *push*. I grabbed the handle, depressed the latch and the door opened. I felt like an idiot. An idiot with a sore shoulder, but an idiot who could still move forward, who was still alive.

"It's okay, you can come," I yelled back at my father, holding the door for him.

My father's head was slightly bowed. He looked as though he was laboring more than he had on the way down the stairs. It must have been like he'd said–on the steps, going down, he'd had gravity working with him. Ting ducked her head slightly to get through the doorframe.

We were standing in a large, carpeted corridor. Again, well lit, and completely deserted. It was as if we were the only people in the whole building, but I knew that wasn't true. The people at this level must have all evacuated. There had to be a mass of bodies below, the stairwells jammed with a crush of people trying to get out. In some ways it would have been good to run into somebody, but I knew it was really better this way. As long as that line kept moving in front of us we were clear to keep moving forward–or, more to the point, down and out.

"Look, elevators!" I exclaimed. I stopped directly in front of the middle of a bank of four. "I just wish we could take these down."

"*You* wish?" my father said, gesturing over his shoulder at Ting.

The scene was so funny that I couldn't help myself and I started to laugh. It was bizarre, unreal, to be standing there laughing, but it felt good.

I stopped myself when I looked down and realized that the carpeting was all discolored in front of two of the elevators, and there was a strange smell . . . a burning smell. And there was something on the floor directly in front of me, a large piece of metal. It looked like . . . it was, the door of one of the elevators!

I took a few steps forward. The entire door of one of the elevators was completely blown off, leaving a big, gaping black hole in its place.

"It must have shot down the elevator shafts," my father said.

"What did?"

"A fireball. That's the only thing that could blow off a metal door. And you can see where it burned the carpet and shot across the lobby. Look at the wall."

Right across from the elevators the wall was scorched and the paint was burned away.

My father swung Ting around, gently placed her on her one good foot and helped her settle to the floor.

"It came through that elevator shaft," my father said.

One of the doors was open a few inches and the shiny metal was brown, scorched around the open edges.

"The jet fuel would have gone to the lowest point, down the shafts, and when it was ignited it would have exploded down those same spots. Anybody in the elevators, anybody standing by an open door would have been–" He stopped.

My mind filled in the rest of the words. They would have been burned to death, incinerated.

I edged away from the opening between the two doors. It was open only a few inches, obviously not enough for me to get through–to *fall* through–but enough to let a deadly stream of fire spew through. Just as bad, it was also open enough to allow my imagination to fit through.

I thought of both the death drop down the black shaft and, more vividly, the searing flames fueled by the jet fuel, flashing out of the shaft and incinerating anything, *anybody* in its path. I stepped past quickly.

That left only the shaft that was completely open. I moved as far away as possible, my shoulder pressed against the far wall. The door was in three pieces, lying on the floor. The wall was scorched from the fire and dented from the force of the door smashing against it. I moved past, not even looking at the hole. My legs felt wobbly. Here I'd been thinking that we were safe, more than a dozen floors removed from the fire, but we weren't. Not here and not now.

Carefully, my father, carrying Ting, moved past the elevator shafts. He stopped just beyond them. Gently he lowered her from his back to the ground.

"There are more stairs, right?" I asked.

"This is a transfer floor," my father said.

"What does that mean?"

"The stairs in this building don't continue all the way straight down. They stop at certain floors, take a jog over and then continue. It's a fire precaution built in by the architects so that smoke can't simply travel all the way up the shaft as if it were a chimney."

"I guess it's good that they did *something* safe," I said, surprised that I was suddenly feeling so angry.

"They did everything they were supposed to do. Nobody could have imagined this happening. It's beyond belief, beyond comprehension. Listen, we'd better get moving again."

My father offered Ting a hand, helping her to her feet. She held her injured leg up so just the very tip of her toe was on the ground. I knew that leg must have hurt, but she wasn't complaining.

"Let me take her," I said.

"Are you sure?"

"I'm sure I want to and sure that I can."

I squatted down in front of her and my father helped her climb on to my back. She wrapped her arms around my neck and I twisted my arms back to support her, locking my fingers together. She was light.

"The stairs are this way." My father led us down another corridor to an exit sign. He opened the door, holding it for me, and then rushed ahead so that he was below us on the stairs. I wasn't planning on falling but it was good to have him there just in case I did.

I concentrated on the steps. I couldn't afford to misstep or stumble. Ting didn't need another knock in the head. Besides, what would happen if I got hurt? It wasn't like my father could carry both of us. Actually, it would have been twice as hard to carry me as it was to carry Ting because I probably outweighed her by eighty pounds.

"You okay?" my father asked.

"Doing okay," I said, trying to control my breath so it wouldn't sound like I was straining. "This is just like football practice."

My father laughed. "I remember that drill from when I played, carrying a teammate across the field."

"We do it the *length* of the field," I said, "and we do it as a race. One guy carries the other one way, and then they switch horse for rider and come back the other way. Last pair have to do forty push-ups, next to last thirty-five, the next team twenty-five and so on. Only the winners are off the hook."

"That's incentive to move fast."

"There are all sorts of incentives to move fast," I said, stating the obvious.

We kept making landings, turning, making floors, turning, heading down. I freed up one hand sometimes to hold on to the railing. It had only been four floors but I was starting to feel it in my lungs and in my legs. I wanted to stop but I didn't. My father had carried her nine floors without stopping. I had to do at least nine . . . no, I had to do at least *ten* floors before I stopped.

My father pulled out his cellphone. I'd forgotten about trying to reach Mom. He punched in the numbers and held it up to his ear.

"Is it ringing?" I asked.

"Nothing, just that fast sort of busy sound you get when you can't get a signal through," he said. "Either the walls of the stairwell are blocking it or there are just so many people trying to phone out that the network is overwhelmed. She must know that the plane hit this building below my floor. Your mother must be just frantic."

I'd been so worried about what was happening with us that I hadn't really thought about what my mother was going through. She got all panicky when I was twenty minutes late for curfew or my father wasn't on the right train. She always worried so much when my father had to fly away on business. She said she didn't trust planes. That was stupid. It was safer to travel by plane than it was by car. Most days. Not today. Not in those two planes.

What would it have been like for those passengers? Would they even have known what was happening? Would they have had any idea that they were about to die? At least it would have been quick. Instant. Not like those people who were trapped by the fire. I could only hope that they'd all be saved, just scared and worried until rescue came. It was better to be worried and alive than oblivious and dead.

"I just pray your mother isn't alone. I hope her sister is there, that she has somebody," my father said.

"Keep on trying to call her." I was finding it tough to find the breath to talk and walk.

"I think the stairwells are cellphone-dead areas. Maybe we should stop and go onto one of the–"

"I don't think we should stop," I said.

"Don't worry. We're safe now." My father sounded supremely confident, almost smug. That tone of his normally just irritated me, mostly because usually he *was* right. This time I just hoped he was.

"I thought we were safe until I saw how the fire traveled down that elevator shaft," I said.

"I'm sure we're safe now."

"We're not stopping," I snapped.

"We're not?" my father asked.

"No. We're going to keep going." That wasn't a suggestion that I was making or something we could debate and decide on. I was going to keep moving whether he liked it or not, whether he agreed or not. I expected my father to say something, to argue–he was used to being the one giving the orders–but I guess he wasn't in the mood for a fight.

"Your mother's always worried when there's nothing to worry about. I guess now she has a reason," my father said.

"But you said you think we're safe here," I said, controlling my breath so I wasn't panting.

"Yes, but she doesn't know that we're here. As far as she's concerned we're still up there, trapped, or worse."

He was right. She would be having a complete meltdown by now.

"I keep trying to remember what the last thing I said to your mother was this morning, before I left."

"I don't understand," I grunted.

"I just can't remember what I said. I can't remember if I told her I loved her or said something nice. I don't remember if I was so busy reading the paper that I didn't pay attention to her over breakfast."

"I don't know what you talked about over breakfast, but I do know you told her you loved her."

"I did? You remember me saying that?" he asked, sounding relieved.

"I don't remember you saying it. I just know that you *always* say it."

He looked back over his shoulder and smiled. "You're right, I do."

He always said it to me, too. I usually just grunted or mumbled goodbye. And I couldn't remember what *I'd* said to Mom. It probably wasn't even a word. I'd been half asleep and not in a great mood to begin with because I didn't want to be awake, never mind heading out the door. When I saw her tonight I'd say something, for sure.

"I just want to get out of the building. We can call Mom when we get out," I said. I took a deep breath. "If we keep moving at this pace we can be out in twenty or thirty minutes."

"You're moving pretty fast," my father said. "Faster than I was going."

"A lot faster," I said.

"Sounds like a challenge."

"Not a challenge, just a fact."

I made the turn to floor fifty-four. That was twelve floors. Three more than my father had managed. I was feeling it even more in my legs and my lungs. It was as if Ting had got heavier with each floor. I didn't know how many more floors I could do. My foot slipped and I stumbled forward, hitting the wall. I grabbed the railing with my free hand and my father reached up and grabbed me with both hands, stopping me before I could tumble down the stairs.

"Thanks," I gasped.

"I think it's time to trade. I'm feeling rested," my father said. He helped Ting off my back. "You lead and I'll carry."

As long as we were moving I didn't care who was doing what. I could take over again in ten or eleven floors.

CHAPTER

TWELVE

"I can take over any time now," I said.

My father had Ting on his back. I was a little worried about him. His face seemed to be getting redder with each floor, and he'd carried her down eleven floors. That was only one less than I'd carried her for. I knew that it was stupid for me to keep track, but I couldn't help it.

"I'll stop . . . at the next floor," he said.

Obviously I wasn't the only one who had been counting.

My father kept moving, and stopped only when we reached the forty-second floor. He slumped down and I helped Ting get off his back. She sagged and I eased her on to the stairs. She hadn't been responding much over the last ten minutes. Her stare was fixed and blank and her body was limp. I wondered if her head injury was more serious than we'd thought. That was even more reason to hurry. I went around in front of Ting so I could pick her up.

"Can you help get her onto my back?" I asked my father.

"Just a minute," my father said. "Let me catch my breath." He was bent over. He did look tired.

"Do you know why I wanted to go one more floor?" he asked.

I knew. It didn't matter, though. Maybe he'd carried her as many floors but I'd done mine faster, I was sure.

"We just passed the halfway mark. Forty-two is less than half of eighty-five, where we started."

I hadn't expected that answer. "That's great."

"Fadder," Ting said, pointing at my dad.

"What?" I asked.

"Fadder." She pointed at him again. Then she pointed at me. "Boy . . . son."

"Oh, yeah, I understand. He's my *father* and I'm his *son*."

She nodded enthusiastically. Then she reached into her pocket and pulled out a wallet. What was she doing? Was she trying to pay us? She pulled out a picture and handed it to me. It was two little girls, wearing matching pink, frilly dresses, their hair in the same braids with identical dark eyes staring out at me. They looked like twins. They couldn't have been more than four or five years old.

"Mudder," Ting said, and touched her hand to her chest.

"Oh, these are your daughters."

She smiled broadly and nodded. "Daughters. Mei-zhen," she said, pointing to one of the girls, "and Ming-zhu," she said as she pointed to the other.

"You have two beautiful girls," my father said. "They'll be very happy to see their mother tonight."

I was struck with a strange thought. If we hadn't heard her call out, if we hadn't found her, then they wouldn't be seeing her tonight. Who knows what would have happened? The fire might have spread, or the roof might have caved in, or something else might have fallen on her. Thank goodness we'd come by.

Then I thought about how I'd wanted to just leave her in the stairwell, how she'd felt like a burden or baggage or, at best, like an unspoken challenge, a competition between me and my father to see who could cart her the farthest.

She was none of those things. She was a real person with at least two other real people–tiny little girls with dark eyes and big smiles–waiting for her at home. They would be happy to see her tonight, they would rush up and throw their arms around her, probably like they did every night when she got home from work. They were so little that it was possible they wouldn't even be aware what was happening or how it might affect their mother and them.

Then I thought about what Mom must be going through, and I flashed forward to how relieved she'd be when she finally heard from us. We had to get down and let her know. She was probably going crazy trying to reach us on my dad's cellphone, not understanding that we were unreachable because we were in the stairwell, not unreachable because . . . because . . .

How many other people were trying to make calls, either out of the building or in? How many people were trying to get confirmation, or reassurance? How many people would never connect again? How many people would never be coming home again? I stopped myself. I couldn't think about that. Not now. Not yet. I felt an ache in my chest thinking about what had happened, wondering how many lives had ended, or been altered forever. All I wanted to do was be home, standing there with my mother, all of us safe.

"Did you hear that?" my father asked.

"Hear what?" I asked, snapping out of my thoughts.

"Maybe I was just hearing things but it sounded like–"

"Voices," I said, cutting him off. I thought that I'd just heard them too. "I think I hear somebody." I listened more closely. I really *wanted* to hear somebody, really *wanted* to see somebody. After traveling over forty floors and finding only Ting, it was starting to feel as if we were the only three people left in the world.

"I think the voices are coming from down below," my father said. "Let's get going and see if we can find them."

I handed Ting her picture and she slipped it back into the wallet.

My father helped Ting get onto my back. She seemed light. Maybe it was because I was rested, or because I was buoyed by the hint of other people being around. Or maybe it was just the challenge of the chase, trying to capture the voices below us.

My father went down the stairs two at a time and I made double time to try to keep up. We practically sprinted down the first two flights. In our rush I couldn't hear anything except the pounding of our feet. We reached the fortieth-floor landing and my father stopped. I skidded in beside him. The voices were there, and they were louder!

"Hello!" my father yelled out down the stairs.

"Hello!" a man's voice answered back. "Where are you?"

"We're on the fortieth floor . . . in the stairwell!"

"We're on the thirty-eighth floor!" the voice called back. "We're coming up!"

Coming up? My father and I exchanged a look of concern. Why would anybody be coming up? They should be heading down . . . unless the way down was blocked. I knew my father was thinking the exact same thing.

My father motioned for me to follow and we headed down the stairs. We reached the first landing and then around the corner and down to the thirty-ninth floor. Now I could clearly hear voices and the sound of feet moving up toward us. There was more than one person.

A man–a *fireman*–appeared on the stairs! He was in full gear and he had an oxygen tank strapped to his back. I felt so incredibly relieved–no, *thrilled*–to see him! Another fireman rounded the corner and then a third and a fourth and a fifth. It was like a whole gang of firefighters . . . no, that wasn't the right word . . . a whole *company* was here to rescue us!

"Are you three all right?" the first fireman asked.

"We're fine," my father said. "Now that we've found you we're *better* than fine."

"Except for Ting," I added. "Her leg is hurt." I gently slipped her off my back to show her leg. She stood gingerly, balanced on her good leg, with me holding her so she wouldn't fall down. I helped her take a seat on the stairs.

"Stein and Galloway, you stay with me," the fireman in charge said to two of the others, "everybody else keep climbing."

Two of the men moved to the side of the stairwell to let the others pass. They were all dressed in full gear–big, black rubber boots, helmets, oxygen tanks–and carrying equipment. There were seven of them, and as they passed I could see that some were straining under the load. They were puffing and huffing and sweat was pouring down their faces.

The first fireman bent down and looked at Ting's leg. "How did it happen?" he asked Ting. His voice was strained.

"She doesn't speak much English," my father explained. "She was injured by a falling cabinet, but I'm more worried about her head. She has a pretty big gash. I think she was hit by a falling piece of ductwork."

The fireman carefully moved the bandana to the side. The other two firemen slumped down to the floor. They were all working to catch their breath, and they were red and sweaty . . . but why shouldn't they be? They'd climbed up almost forty stories while carrying full equipment! They looked exhausted, and they were still less than halfway to the fire. What shape would any of them be when they finally got there?

A loud burst of static came from a radio clipped to the jacket of one of the firemen. I didn't really understand what the person on the other end was saying.

"That cut is pretty bad. She needs to be treated," the fireman said. "There are ambulances waiting below."

"Have a lot of people been hurt?" I asked.

"There have been many casualties, but it's being handled. Can you two continue to take her down?" he asked my father.

"You mean you're not going to take care of her?" I asked.

He shook his head. "We're going up, not down. We have to keep moving toward the people at the top, toward the fire. Either she has to wait here for paramedics to arrive or you have to take her down. Can you at least take her down until you find a paramedic?"

"We're not leaving her behind," my father said firmly.

"We'll get her all the way to the lobby if we have to," I said.

"That's thirty-nine floors."

"We can do it. We've been taking turns carrying her and we've already brought her down over forty floors," my father said.

"Forty floors? Where exactly did you three come from?"

"We found Ting on the seventy-fifth floor," my father said. "But we came down from the eighty-fifth floor, my office. That was where we were when the plane hit."

"That means you were *above* the point of impact." It sounded as though the fireman couldn't believe his ears.

My father nodded. "We were a few floors above. It looked like it was worst around the seventy-eighth floor to the eightieth floor."

"But you got past those floors."

"It wasn't easy."

"Do you know if anybody else came through that way?"

"We don't know. We just know that nobody came down with us. Before we tried to head down we saw people going *up* in Stairwell B. Those people said that the stairwell going down was blocked. There was smoke and heat, but the way we came down, in Stairwell A, it was passable. At least it was when we went through."

"But this is Stairwell C," the fireman said.

"We were in A until we came to the transfer hall on the sixty-sixth floor and then we just took the first stairs we could find from there," my father explained.

"And it's just the three of you?" the fireman asked. "Have you seen anybody else?"

"We haven't been checking the floors on the way down but we haven't seen or heard anybody, other than Ting, since we left our floor."

"And what about the rest of the people who were on your floor, what happened to them?"

"I'm the fire warden on eighty-five. When the first plane hit I ordered my office to evacuate and I went to the other offices on the floor to order them out."

"You got the whole floor cleared?"

"I'm so sorry. I couldn't get one office to leave. They were still there when the second plane hit."

"And then?"

"They joined other people from the lower floors who were climbing away from the fire. They were all going to the top."

"Maybe they found another way down," I said. "We were thinking that maybe they could have been taken off by helicopters."

"There have been no air evacs. There's too much smoke to put down. People are only getting down if we can get up and get them down," he said.

"Can you get word to the people at the top and let them know it was possible to get down the way we did?" my father said.

"They'll radio down to the command post and then they'll pass on the information. You three go slowly, take your time and get out safely."

"Thanks . . . we will," my father said. "We were wondering, is it clear all the way down?"

"No worries. The stairs are open and clear. You'll only run into a few stragglers still getting down. People moved pretty quickly, very orderly," the fireman said. "It was like a gigantic school fire drill. I was impressed by how well people handled it. The only ones still on the stairs are those who are physically challenged . . . old or overweight or disabled."

"Plus a few people who refused to leave at first," one of the other firemen added.

"Can you believe that?" the third fireman asked. "The building has been hit by an airplane, it's on fire, and some people want to stay hunched over their computer terminals working."

"You know what they call a guy who isn't smart enough to leave a burning building?" one of the firemen asked.

"They call him a fireman," the second said, and they all started to laugh.

"We gotta get going." The two firemen struggled under the weight of their equipment and got to their feet.

"Take it carefully, slow and easy," one of them said to us.

I felt like saying the same thing to them.

We stood off to the side to allow them to get by us. They probably had as much weight on their backs as we did when we were carrying Ting, and we were heading *down* the stairs and alternating having her on our backs. I watched until the last man turned the corner and was gone.

My father helped Ting first to her feet and then up onto my back. We started down again. I felt so much better than I had just a few minutes ago. It wasn't just being told that the way was clear all the way down, it was knowing that there was a whole group of firefighters who were now positioned between the danger and us. Not only weren't we alone, but we had them there to take care of the situation.

"You know, when I was in my teens I wanted to be a fireman," my father said.

"You did?"

"You sound surprised. I think every little boy wants to be a firefighter at some point. Didn't you?"

"Yeah . . . when I was about six."

He laughed. "I even talked to my guidance counselor about what I'd have to study after high school. She told me, but really she spent most of the time trying to talk me out of it."

"Looks like it worked."

"It did, and I guess I'm grateful."

"You certainly can't earn the money you earn being a firefighter," I said.

"Money isn't everything."

I wanted to say something but I kept my mouth shut. Money meant a big house and fancy cars and skiing holidays and all those other things that somebody on a firefighter's salary couldn't afford–things I knew James's family didn't have. Sometimes I even felt bad about that, sort of guilty for having more than he did. I couldn't help but think how different our lives would have been if my father *had* been a fireman. We certainly wouldn't have had as much . . . at least not as many possessions.

"There are lots of rewards that have nothing to do with money when you do a job like that," my father said. "I can only imagine the way it would feel to save somebody's life."

I thought about Ting on my back. Maybe he didn't have to imagine that hard.

"Nobody ever has a bad thing to say about firefighters," my father continued. "They're like knights in shining armor riding to the rescue. Instead of a white stallion they have red–"

My father stopped talking. He'd heard the same voices I had. Somebody else was coming up the stairs. We turned the corner and bumped into another group of firefighters climbing up. Dressed in their special suits, tanks on their backs, axes in their belts, they did look like they were wearing suits of armor.

"How are you doing?" the fireman in the lead asked.

"We're good," my father said. "We just passed ten of your–"

"John! Will!"

It was Mr. Bennett, James's father!

"I'm so happy to see you two!" he exclaimed. He stopped, but the rest of the firefighters with him kept climbing. I pressed as close to the side of the stairs as I could to allow them to pass by.

"I knew you worked in one of these buildings but I didn't know which one or what floor. I just knew you were here today, and Will was with you."

"We're okay," I said. "We're just moving slowly because we have to take turns carrying Ting."

He nodded his head. "I should have figured that you two would have been helping instead of needing help. Can you do me a favor?"

"As long as it doesn't involve carrying anybody else," my father joked.

"Not carrying, but bringing. James is back at the station and I'm gonna be here all night. All emergency personnel in the whole city are on twenty-four-hour call. I can't be going off duty until at least sometime tomorrow. I didn't want James to go home alone, and it's going to be almost impossible for his mother to get into the city because roads and bridges are closed to incoming traffic. Do you think you could pass by the station–it's only two blocks down–and bring him home with you?"

"Of course we can. It's the least we can do for one of New York's bravest. We'll take care of James and you take care of this building."

He smiled. "Thanks. He'll be happy to know that you're safe, and it'll take a weight off my mind. I'd better get going." He shook my father's hand again and then came up to my level. "Tell my kid not to worry . . . okay?"

"I'll tell him." I knew I would try to say the words, but I wasn't sure how honest it was to reassure James when his father was heading deliberately toward the danger we were trying so hard to escape. I had to wonder then if this was the sort of worry that James lived with every day.

"Good." He started up the stairs at double-time, trying to catch up with his company. He turned the corner and was gone, although I could still hear his boots pounding against the stairs.

"You okay to keep carrying Ting or do you want me take over for a while?" my father asked.

"Let me go one more, to the thirtieth floor, and then you can take over," I said. I wanted to do my twelve floors.

CHAPTER THIRTEEN

"I'm not quite keeping the same pace as you," my father said

"Not quite, but not bad . . . for an old man."

He chuckled. "I guess I'm old compared to you. How is Ting doing?" he asked.

She hadn't said a word for a long time. I looked up. Her eyes were closed. Was she sleeping? Was she unconscious? I reached up and gently shook her shoulder.

"Ting?" I asked.

Her eyes slowly opened. She smiled.

"Are you okay?" I remembered that was one of the words she knew.

"Okay . . . tired."

Tired? She was the one being carried, not the one doing the carrying.

"That's a symptom of concussion," my father explained. "We have to keep her awake. It's not good for a concussion victim to go to sleep. Ting!" My father's voice was loud and she jumped a little in response. "You have to stay awake!"

She looked more awake, but more confused than anything else.

"We'd better hurry," I said, and we started down the stairs again.

"I have to tell you, in a funny way, I'm grateful you're here," my father said.

"You are?" I questioned. "I thought you wanted me to be somewhere else, anywhere else except here."

"I did, I *do*, but I don't know what would have happened if you hadn't been with me."

That seemed like a weird thing to say, all things considered. But there was one obvious reason why he was glad.

"It sure would have been hard to carry Ting all that way by yourself," I agreed.

"I may not have even found her without you."

"But you heard her calling too," I said.

"I only heard her because we went down the stairs. If you hadn't been with me, I might have gone up, instead."

"But *I* was the one who wanted to go up. It was *your* idea, *your* decision, to head down." I didn't add that I'd thought it was a bad idea at the time.

"It *was* my idea, but the only reason I made that decision was because of you. If it had been just me, I might have gone with everybody else up to the roof and waited it out," my father said. "But because I had you with me I couldn't risk that. I had to take the chance to try to get down."

"I don't get it."

"And you probably won't until you have kids of your own," he said.

"What does that mean?"

"You'd risk your life for your kids, give up your life for your kids without even having to think about it. I had to take that risk in going down. Do you understand now?"

"I guess. But you had me go with you–wasn't that putting *my* life at risk?"

"A calculated risk, but that's why I went down first. If something happened to me, I hoped you'd still be able to go back up the stairs. Nothing in this entire world, nothing, is as important as you."

I felt embarrassed hearing him say that. Would I be willing to give up my life for him? I thought I might . . . but I'd definitely have to think about it before I made that decision. I was uncomfortable and wanted to change the subject.

"Who do you think did it?" I asked.

"What?" my father asked, sounding confused.

"Who do you think it was that did this . . . that crashed the planes?"

"Oh . . . oh. My guess would be Muslim extremists. At least, those were the people responsible for the World Trade Center bombing in 1993."

"That's right, I'd sort of forgotten about that."

"You were pretty young at the time, but believe me, *I'll* never forget it."

"Were you in here when it happened?" I asked.

"It was in the underground parking garage, closer to the North Tower, but I was here, in this building, just heading out for lunch. It was around twenty minutes after twelve, Friday, February twenty-sixth."

"You remember the date?"

"I told you, I'll never forget."

"What exactly happened?" I asked.

"A truck was parked in the underground garage. It contained fifteen hundred pounds of explosive. The explosion created a crater five stories deep and twenty-two feet wide."

"Wow, that's unbelievable. How many people were hurt?"

"Six deaths and over a thousand people injured. I'm afraid that's going to pale compared to today. I don't even want to think about how many people have died . . . or are going to die."

"It's awful . . . even more awful that it had to happen here twice. That doesn't seem fair."

"Not fair, but deliberate. This is an attack on one of the most important, most visible symbols of the United States. This isn't just a building, the World Trade Center represents the United States of America."

"But why would anybody want to do this to us? What did we do that could cause somebody to hate our country that much?" I asked.

"Different people have different theories. Some people–simple people–say things like, 'Those people hate freedom' or 'They're jealous because we have so much.'"

"But you don't agree?"

"I agree we have a lot, a lot more than almost everybody in the whole world, but that isn't it. There are other countries that have the same standard of living as us–countries like Sweden, Switzerland, Germany . . . or Canada, but nobody hates Canada. And it certainly isn't just about freedom, because all of those countries are as free and democratic as us."

"Then what is it?"

"I think it isn't what we *are* but what we *represent*. We're the only true world power left. The United States is the dominant economic, cultural and military power on the planet. So every time something goes wrong, or doesn't go the way it's supposed to go, then we're the ones who take the blame."

"What do you mean?"

"If two countries in Africa are at war, then half the world is angry because we haven't sent troops in to police, patrol and settle the dispute."

"Do people really expect us to do that?" I asked.

"A whole lot of countries. Unfortunately, if we *do* send in our soldiers, then the other half of the world is mad at us for interfering."

"So you think no matter what we do we're going to be blamed, that it isn't our fault."

"I'm saying that, but I'm also *not* saying that."

I didn't understand.

"Sometimes we aren't as sensitive as we could be to other cultures, and let's be honest, sometimes we do act to protect our interests in ways that might not necessarily be in the best interests of other countries. But still, we don't deserve this . . . nobody deserves this."

"Why do these Muslims act that way? Why are they so filled with hate?" I asked.

"First off, it might not even be Muslims," he said. "Look at the Oklahoma City bombing, that was home-grown American citizens. And second, I didn't say Muslims, I said Muslim *extremists.*" He stopped talking to catch his breath. I knew how hard it was to walk, carry Ting and talk. "Most Muslims–heck most Christians, Jews, Hindus and Buddhists–are peaceful people."

"But I keep hearing on the news about Muslims in the Middle East blowing themselves up and killing innocent people," I said.

"Extremists. People who don't really understand what their own religion is about. Can you imagine any person, any normal, any religious person, saying they want to kill innocent people?"

"Not really but–" I stopped. I heard more voices coming up the stairs toward us.

"I think it's more emergency personnel," my father said. "I can hear their radios."

I could hear those static-filled voices too. I was hoping it was firefighters and not paramedics. We'd worked too hard and taken Ting too far to stop now–unless she needed us to stop. Did she need to have a paramedic examine her right now?

I looked up at her. Her eyes were open and she smiled at me. That was reassuring, but if these were paramedics we'd stop and have her seen.

The voices, the radios, were getting louder and louder. I turned the corner. It was firefighters, but they weren't climbing, they were sitting at the bottom of the next landing. What were they doing? One of them was practically lying down and his shirt was off and the others were giving him oxygen!

I slowed down and we came to a stop a few steps above them. The man's face was as white as snow, there were beads of sweat pouring down his forehead and his eyes were closed . . . was he . . . was he . . . No, I could see his chest moving up and down.

One of the firefighters looked up. "Just slip on by," he said.

I wanted to ask if he was okay, to say something, but there was nothing I could say. Slowly, cautiously, I stepped onto the landing, trying not to look at him, but being careful not to step on anything or anybody.

One of the firemen was practically yelling into his radio, trying to let them know what was happening, trying to get a paramedic up to assist.

I started down to the next landing. I turned back around to make sure my father was able to get by safely. He slipped by. He nodded to me reassuringly, to let me know he was fine, to let me know that everything was fine . . . even though I knew it wasn't.

CHAPTER FOURTEEN

Floor eighteen. We were getting closer. Each step, each turn, each floor, we were getting closer. We'd been passed by dozens and dozens of police and firefighters now, and two paramedics. They'd done a quick check of Ting and then rushed off to help that poor fireman.

The firefighters–all of the emergency people–were rushing up the stairs, toward what everybody else had been rushing away from. Just like James's dad. What made a person do something like that? What kind of person had that sort of guts? I looked at my father, moving down the stairs in front of me. He'd wanted to be a fireman. Could

I picture him doing that, risking his own life for other people? I didn't have to look–or *feel*–beyond Ting on my back to know the answer to that. He would have been a very good fireman.

As we'd continued down we'd also come across some of the people who were still straggling out of the building. There was the very, very large woman who was sitting on the stairs when we got to her. With her was a younger woman, trying to convince her that she needed to go on, that she could reach the bottom if she only got up and tried.

There were two older men, guided by a younger man, who were coming down very, very slowly. One of them was friendly and joking around and talked to us as we passed. He offered to carry Ting *and* my father, if we needed help. The other was just old and cranky and complained about how they should let him use the elevator.

Then there were four men, taking turns in pairs to carry a man in a wheelchair. They'd go a floor at a time, then trade. The man wasn't small, and between him and the chair it made carrying Ting seem like nothing.

I was tired, and it wasn't like I didn't know she was there, but I also knew we could do it, we could make it.

"I'd love to have a cold beer right about now," my father said.

"Me too."

He gave me a funny look.

"Just kidding, but a cold Coke, on ice, in a big chilled glass would go down real well," I said.

"Actually, that sounds better than a beer. A glass of water would be best. I'm really thirsty."

"I could go for that," I said. "I'm glad you told me to take that drink of water up in your office."

He looked back up at me and smiled. "You know, when I see you, I'm almost a little shocked. You just seem so big, so old. It was like one day you were this little boy and I turned away for a few seconds and when I looked again you were a strapping young man."

I wanted to tell him that he'd turned away for years, but I didn't say anything. This wasn't the time to pick a fight. I knew he was trying to say something.

"I guess, really, I turned away for more than a few seconds," he said.

I was thrown by that–it was as though he had just read my mind.

"Business has taken me away more than it should have," he continued. "And I don't just mean on business trips or long hours at the office. Sometimes even when I'm home my mind is somewhere else. I guess I could have been a better father."

I didn't answer.

"This is where you're supposed to say that it's okay and that I *was* a good father," he said.

"You were a good father . . . especially when I was little."

"I guess you're right, I was better when you were little. And you know what? I'd rather you were honest about that instead of lying. It would have been easy to lie, so I'm glad you didn't."

I knew my father was waiting for me to say something, but I really didn't know what to say.

"Do you know why your mother thinks you and I fight and argue?" he asked.

"Because we're so much alike."

"She told you, too, huh?" he asked.

"More than once."

"And do you agree with her?"

"How could we *not* have some things in common?" I asked.

"One of the biggest things I see is that we're both really competitive," he said.

"Nothing wrong with that."

"Sometimes there is. I think that need to compete is what got in my way. Business isn't about money. Money is just how you keep score of who's winning. There was always some deal that had to be done, something that seemed so urgent, so big, that I lost sight of the really important things."

I knew my father was trying to apologize, but this was really hard to talk about. I needed to change the subject.

"Can I ask you a question?" I asked.

"Of course."

"When we started to carry Ting you always thought, right from the beginning, that we were going to carry her all the way down, didn't you?"

"Am I that predictable?"

"I just knew. That's part of you being competitive."

"I guess it is," he admitted. "And that's just like you making sure you always carried her more floors than I did."

I felt myself blush.

"Not that that was bad either. It helped us keep moving."

"I guess so," I admitted.

"Besides, doesn't it say something that I knew how many floors we were each carrying her?" he asked with a chuckle.

"I guess it does. Can I ask you one more question?"

"Shoot."

"Did you have a deadline in mind–you know, were you trying to get out of the building before a certain time?"

"At first," he said, "I was just hoping we *would* get out of the building. I really had my doubts we could get past those floors."

"I know," I said.

"I tried to hide it. I didn't want to worry you any more than you already were."

"I don't know if that would have been possible," I said, although his being calm had certainly made me feel better. "But after we got past the flames and we found Ting, *then* did you have a time that you were trying to beat?"

He smiled. "I was shooting for ten-thirty."

"We're going to beat that easily. We're going to be out by ten."

"We will if we hurry."

"Not we. You." I stopped at the eighth-floor landing. "It's your turn."

I helped slide Ting off my back and onto her feet. I looked at my watch. It was eleven minutes to ten. We *could* do it before ten. I helped Ting up and on to my father's back.

I started down the stairs. All we had to do was travel one flight per minute and we'd beat 10:00. I deliberately set a fast pace. My father was right on my heels. We hit the seventh floor and I looked at my watch. Less than forty-five seconds. That made me feel good.

My legs felt light. The sense of being tired, of wearing down, was all gone. This was the end. Just a few more flights and it would all be over. I almost felt like laughing out loud.

The sixth floor flashed by, then the fifth, and I turned for the fourth. At the corner we came across a group of police officers climbing up.

"How's it going?" the first cop said as he passed by.

"Good. We're almost out," I said.

"You want one of us to help with her?" he asked my father.

"No," my father said. "It's all under control." He didn't even break pace or slow down.

The officers passed us on the left. The last in line was older and more than a little overweight. He was already puffing and huffing and falling behind the other three. I didn't want to think of what might happen to him. I had visions of that fireman being given oxygen and wondered how he was doing. He was still up there somewhere, although he might only be a few floors and a few minutes behind us.

"We've come this far," my father said to me. "We started and we're going to finish."

We passed by the third-floor landing. The door was open. I glanced in as I passed. The lights were on and everything looked normal, as if nothing had happened. I continued down for the second floor. We were actually going faster, as though we were gaining momentum as we got closer to the ground.

"Am I going too fast?" I asked as I hit the landing.

"Just the right speed."

I made the turn at the next landing and stopped. Down below was a long, long, straight flight of stairs. At the very end was an open door and there was bright light. It was the lobby!

"Wait," my father said. "Do you want to carry Ting the last few steps?"

"I can if you need a break."

"I don't need a break," he said. "I just thought you'd like to finish."

It was a nice offer. "It doesn't matter who's carrying her at the end," I said. "We did it together. Let's just get it done."

We started down the stairs–the last flight of stairs. It was long and straight, and as I neared the bottom I could hear voices, lots of voices. I could almost visualize a ribbon stretched across the doorway, the finish line. Just a few more steps. I wanted to raise my hands into the air and scream and–I skidded to a stop. I couldn't believe what I saw.

We were standing on the terrace above the lobby, the mezzanine. Twenty or thirty feet below us was the lobby.

"Oh my God," my father said as he stopped beside me.

This couldn't be the same place we'd walked through just a couple of hours before. Had it really been only a couple of hours? It seemed more like days. The whole lobby was littered with shattered glass and chunks of marble and concrete. All around the debris were police and firefighters and paramedics. They were talking on phones and radios, treating injured people, helping other stragglers, directing them out of the building.

Two paramedics and a police officer rushed over to our side.

"Here, let us help you," one of the paramedics said. The other helped Ting down and the two of them started to move her.

"No! No!" she protested, fighting them, struggling to get back to where my father and I stood.

I hadn't expected her to do that, to fight against them. She looked scared, panicky.

"It's okay, Ting," my father said. He moved to her side and she threw an arm around his shoulders, breaking free of the paramedics.

"We're not going to hurt you," one of the paramedics said to her.

"We just want to get her on to a stretcher and into one of the ambulances," the other said.

"She doesn't speak much English," my father explained.

"Can you translate for us?" the paramedic asked.

"I don't speak whatever language she speaks," my father said.

"I don't understand anything except English, but I do understand that she doesn't seem to want to leave the two of you," the other paramedic said.

"We've come a long way together," my father explained. I thought that was a pretty big understatement.

"How about if you go a little bit farther. Can you stay here, let us do a preliminary examination, and then you can take her to one of the ambulances? They're waiting just outside across the plaza."

"Sure," my father said. He turned to me. "What time is it?"

"Two minutes to ten."

He smiled. "Tell you what. You go out and give your mother a call. She must be worried sick. I'll meet you right by the ambulances."

I hesitated for a split second. I didn't want to leave him behind, even for a minute, but I did want to finally get out of the building, and we did need to let Mom know we were okay, let her know as soon as possible.

My father handed me his cellphone. "Go . . . don't worry," he said, reading my expression.

I nodded my head. "You'll be right behind me, right?"

"Right behind you. Go, call your mother, she needs to know we're coming home."

"Come this way," the police officer said.

The officer took me by the arm and led me along the mezzanine. I looked out at the plaza and saw a scene as devastated as the lobby. There were hunks of metal and concrete peppering the plaza.

"Don't look," the officer said. "There's no point in looking."

He led me down the escalator. It wasn't working and it felt awkward stumbling down the unevenly spaced stairs. He guided me across the lobby.

"Come on, kid, this is the way out . . . the safe way out. Too much falling from the sky on the other sides."

We stepped out through what had been a floor-to-ceiling window, the remains crunching under our feet.

"Wait," the officer said. There was another officer standing just outside the window. He was looking up.

"Is it clear?" the policeman with me yelled out.

The second officer didn't look our way. He just nodded. "Go and go fast."

The officer took my arm and we started across the plaza. I knew better than to look up. I knew what could be coming down from the sky. I hurried along with him and then tripped over a piece of the building that had fallen and created a divot in the concrete of the plaza. His hands kept me from falling.

And then I thought about those two people, flying past the window. They would have landed–not here, but between the two towers. I couldn't even imagine what would happen to a human body that fell from that height . . . or a human body that was hit by somebody falling from that height. I tried not to think about any of that. I looked straight ahead of me.

There were emergency vehicles everywhere. Fire trucks and police cars were haphazardly parked with flashing lights blazing. Behind them was a row of waiting ambulances, their lights flashing too. With each step I was getting closer to them, closer to safety. We had to be far enough away now to be free of anything falling.

For the first time I looked back, over my shoulder, and let my eyes follow up the smooth glass skin of the towers. It all looked unremarkable until the very top, where thick black smoke poured out and stained the sky. There was a helicopter–no *two* helicopters circling around. For a split second I thought they might be pulling people off the roof. Then I remembered what I'd heard, and what I was seeing with my own eyes. There was no way they could set down through all that smoke. They weren't there to rescue but to witness, watching the scene and probably beaming out TV signals that were circling the globe. How unreal would it seem to those people watching from their homes? How unreal it seemed to me, and I was right there, living through it . . . living through it . . . that was right . . . I *had* lived through it.

"It's like a war zone," the officer said.

"What?" I asked, turning toward him.

"A war zone, like something from a movie, not something that could be happening in New York."

"Not something that could happen anywhere. I just can't believe it."

"Me neither, kid, me neither. The ambulances are right there. You head on over and I'd better get back inside. You make your phone call. Your mom must be scared to death, worrying. This is going to be the nicest phone call she ever gets in her entire life."

That thought made me smile. The officer started back to the building and I pulled the cellphone out of my pocket. I'd just go over and stand by the ambulances and wait for my father.

I dialed the first three numbers, hoping I'd be able to get through this time. I stopped dialing and walking . . . there was a sound . . . like thunder . . . but there wasn't a cloud . . . As I craned my neck to see the top of the building it sagged and it started to collapse!

CHAPTER

FIFTEEN

I turned and started to run when all at once I was picked up and thrown, sailing, through the air. I skidded into the pavement, my face crashing into the concrete! My head and my back and legs were stung by the bite of something smashing into them. I tried to pull my arms over my head and I was engulfed in a thick, white cloud of dust, stinging my eyes, choking my lungs as my ears were flooded with sounds so intense it felt as if my eardrums might burst. The sounds went on and on and on, and then, it all just stopped.

I struggled to get to my feet but couldn't and fell back down to my knees. I tried to draw in a breath but it was as if I were lying face first in sand–the harder I tried, the more the dust was drawn into my lungs. I felt as if I were drowning in the air. I pushed off with my hands and staggered to my feet. I tried to see through the cloud . . . tried to understand what had happened . . . what was happening. I coughed violently, trying desperately to expel dust and gather air into my lungs. I looked back and peered through the cloud . . . it was so thick I couldn't even see the building . . . I tripped over something and smashed back down to the ground.

My ears became filled with the sound of sirens, as thick in my ears as the dust was in my throat. I knew something had fallen–maybe the entire top of the building–sending up the cloud of swirling, choking, blinding dust so thick that it blocked everything from my view. I couldn't even see the tower. Maybe I wasn't even looking in the right direction any more. I hardly knew which way was down. I tried to look up, to see the sky, but all I could make out was a sort of brightness in the white cloud where the sun was trying to force its way through. I staggered a few feet in one direction and then the other, going nowhere. Where was there to go? Which direction should I head? I tripped and fell down again. What had I tripped over? It was a gigantic piece of concrete. If that had hit me I would have been crushed, my head broken into little pieces, killed.

I scrambled forward on all fours. Through the haze I could see that the ground was littered with pieces of concrete, hunks of metal, broken and shattered shards of glass. I looked down at my hands. They were white and red! The palms of both hands were cut and bleeding, the left hand worse than the right. It was bleeding badly, blood flowing out of a large, ugly gash that extended up from my hand to my elbow. My shirt was shredded and torn. I held my arm up and slowly turned it around, looking at the cut, watching the blood dripping out of it. It didn't hurt. There was no feeling . . . it was just numb . . . like I felt. This was unreal, like a dream . . . a nightmare.

The white cloud was streaked with bursts of red and yellow pulsating, flashing lights, from the roofs of the emergency vehicles. The lights met and passed and parted and joined. They were coming from all over, creating a strange, bizarre light show.

I became aware of people all around me, running, screaming. They looked more like ghosts, faces and clothes covered with the thick white powder. I struggled to my feet again, my knees shaking, not sure if I could walk even if I did know which way to go.

Suddenly I was hit from behind and knocked off my feet.

"I'm so sorry!" a man yelled. He grabbed my arm and helped me up. It was a police officer. He was covered from head to toe in dust, his hat missing, his eyes wide open, dark holes staring out at me from a blanket of white. He looked terrified.

"You gotta move away!" he screamed. "Get away!"

"I have to wait here for my father!"

"Your father . . . where's your father?"

"He's in the lobby."

"The lobby . . . the lobby of what?"

"The South Tower."

He seemed to recoil in shock. "Oh, son . . . I'm so sorry . . . so sorry."

"So sorry about what?" I demanded.

"It's gone."

"Gone? What do you mean gone?"

"The building, the whole building, the South Tower, it's gone, it collapsed."

"It can't be gone! It can't! You're wrong!"

"We have to move away. Come on, let me get you to an ambulance. You have to be treated."

"I have to find my father!" I screamed.

"There's nothing that we can do son, we just have to–"

"Leave me alone!" I yelled, and I tried to break away from his grip on my arm. "I've got to find my father!"

He held me tight and I thrashed around, breaking his hold. He tried to grab me again and I stumbled away, forward, in the direction I thought was toward the building. I got no more than a half dozen steps when I crashed over top of something and flew forward, landing painfully on my hands and knees.

A firm hand grabbed me by the shoulder and pulled me to my feet. It was the officer again.

"You have to come with me, there's no choice."

"But I can see it! I can see the building!" I said, pointing through the cloud.

A dark shadow could be seen through the cloud. It was the tower . . . but it looked different . . . the shape was all wrong. I strained my eyes, trying to make sense of what I was seeing. It had a jagged outline . . . oh my God . . . it wasn't the tower . . . it was the *remains* of the tower . . . a twisted tangle of metal and concrete that had collapsed, throwing rubble across the plaza. The building was gone. My father was gone.

My knees felt like rubber, and if it hadn't been for the officer's hand holding me up I might have fallen again. Then I had the strangest thought . . . that nursery rhyme from history class . . . *we all fall down . . . we all fall down*. The words echoed in my head.

"Come on, son, we have to move farther away. It's not safe here."

He started to lead me away. I was powerless to stop him . . . but why would I even try? I looked back over my shoulder. I could make out the images of people, stumbling around in the thick white cloud. They were lost, confused, unsure where to go, possibly–probably–hurt or injured, definitely stunned, unable to comprehend what they had just witnessed, what they'd just been a part of.

I suddenly dug in my heels and stopped.

"We have to keep moving," the officer said. "It isn't safe here."

"No." I reached down. Still around my neck was the string holding the whistle. I put it to my lips and began blowing. It made a shrill call that sounded so loud in my ears but was absorbed and silenced by the dust and the sounds all around me. I kept on blowing anyway, expelling every last bit of air I had in my lungs into that whistle. He'd told me he'd come if I blew the whistle . . . he promised . . . he promised . . .

I began coughing. The dust replaced the air.

"He said he'd come if I whistled," I cried, desperately trying to explain it to the officer. "He said he'd come."

The policeman placed an arm around my shoulders. "He can't hear you, son. We have to go . . . we have to . . . your father would have wanted you to be safe."

I felt my whole body get weak. My father would have wanted me to . . .

I saw a figure, slowly moving forward, too tall to be real . . . no, not one figure, *two* . . . one person carrying another!

I broke away from the officer, my movement so sudden and unexpected that he couldn't stop me.

I ran, closing the gap, hoping, praying, hearing the officer screaming for me to come back, but I kept on running and then skidded to a stop. It was my father, although I almost didn't recognize him. He was covered with a thick layer of white dust and his clothes were practically shredded and hanging from his body. There was blood streaming down from his forehead. Ting still clung tightly to his back, her black eyes staring out in shock and surprise.

"Will!"

I threw my arms around him. "You're okay . . . you're . . ."

"I'm okay."

"I thought you were dead." I burst into tears.

"It's all right. I'm alive. We're *all* alive. I heard the whistle."

I hugged him with all my might. Then an arm wrapped around me. I looked up and realized it was Ting's arm around my shoulders.

"We had just left the building and we were picked up and thrown, like rag dolls, by this rush of air . . . the building just collapsed and shot us out of the way. I was slammed into the ground, and when I was able to get air back into my lungs I realized that Ting was still on my back. I crawled, scrambled away, with her still there."

"Come on, all of you, we have to leave, we can't stay here!" It was the police officer.

"This is my *father*," I said. "And *now* we can go."

AUTHOR NOTE

I was sitting in my little office in the basement of my house, working away on a novel, when my wife called me on the phone. She said I had to turn on the TV. Something had happened—something terrible—in New York City. I flipped on the set and was greeted by an image that was incredibly disturbing and completely unbelievable. The screen showed one of the towers of the World Trade Center, ablaze, smoke pouring out of a gigantic gash in its side.

The announcer said that they were still gathering information, but from what they knew, a plane—a large commercial jet—had crashed into the building. They were still trying to piece together what had happened and what was going to happen next.

As I sat there, eyes glued to the screen, not able to fully understand the scale of the tragedy, a dark shade, a second plane, streaked across the sky and sliced into the other tower, disappearing, transformed into a gigantic orange ball of flames and fire. I felt as if my heart had stopped beating. I blinked. I rubbed my eyes. This couldn't be happening. This couldn't be real. This was too awful to even imagine, and now it was playing out before my eyes—before the eyes of the world—on CNN.

I sat there for the rest of the day, watching first one tower and then the second tumble down. I watched as the scene shifted to the Pentagon. I heard reports about the plane being downed in Pennsylvania, and how all flights in the United States were being suspended, while midair flights were being diverted to Canada.

It was at that time that I heard the sound of an airplane right over top of my house. It got louder and louder—disturbingly loud. What was a plane doing flying so low? The worst possible thoughts flooded my mind. I rushed outside as the craft flew over my house. It was an air-ambulance helicopter setting down at the local hospital. For a few seconds I had thought the worst instead of the usual.

I didn't write any more that day. Ironically, the story I was writing involved a group of terrorists trying to kidnap two young members of Britain's royal family. I didn't write again for weeks. My soul and my psyche were both too distracted, too troubled, too disturbed. The terrible enormity of what had happened was all just too much. I'd be walking the dog, eating a meal, or waking up and I'd just feel . . . *off*. I didn't know what, but something just wasn't *right*.

Then I'd remember, and I'd know what was wrong. For a while I wondered if those feelings would ever go away. Slowly, ever so slowly, they faded.

I lived my life, the way all people had to go on with their lives. I began to write again, first working on the novel I was creating at the time, and then another one, and another and another. Sometimes, during school visits, I would be asked if I thought I would ever write a story about 9/11. I always answered that I thought maybe, at some point, perhaps . . . but I really didn't think I would. I wasn't sure if I could ever put into words what I'd witnessed, what I'd been a part of from six hundred miles away. Two years after 9/11 I was still being asked that same question. Something about what had happened was very much alive in the minds of the students. They needed to know more. And maybe I needed to write the story, my way, in my words.

What happened in New York and Washington and Pennsylvania were attacks against the United States of America. But they were more than that. They were atrocities against all good-thinking people, of all countries, of all faiths. This book is my way, my small way, of helping me, and others, to come to grips with this evil and to emphasize that, as Gandhi said, in the end, good always triumphs.

ABOUT THE AUTHOR

Eric Walters, a former elementary-school teacher, began writing as a way to encourage his students to become more enthusiastic about literature. His many works include *Camp X*, *Royal Ransom*, and *Run*. His novels have won numerous awards including the Silver Birch, Blue Heron, Red Maple, Snow Willow, and Ruth Schwartz, and have received honours from the Canadian Library Association Book of the Year, and UNESCO's international award for Literature in Service of Tolerance. He lives in Mississauga, Ontario.